Lilac Blossom Diaries

By

Mary Mullett-Flynn

Copyright©2016 by Mary Mullett-Flynn

Lilac Blossom Diaries

ISBN #1534621180

All rights reserved. No part of this book may be used or reproduced or transmitted in any form or by any means, electronical or mechanical, including photocopying, recording or by any information storage and retrieval system, without the permission in writing from the publisher, except in case of brief quotations embodied in critical articles and reviews

Printed in the United States

This book is dedicated to

My Heart-Patrick
My children -Maggie, Dave, Sean, Melissa and Evan
My grandchildren - Avery and Emmett
My Mother-in-law - Suzanne Marvin Flynn
The blossoms in my garden

Acknowledgements

I would like to acknowledge the enormous and generous amount of support, love and patience I have received from family and friends:

In 1991 my husband, Patrick left a note for me one morning.

Mary,
Just a note to say I love you. I have great faith in your ability to become a successful writer or whatever you want to become. Because Mary, you are the greatest.
Love,
Patrick

My thanks to my children, Maggie & Dave Farley, Sean & Melissa Flynn and Evan Flynn for the love, laughter and support they always give to me, and my grandchildren, Avery & Emmett Farley for their smiles and laughter.
The Harbor Girls: Lois Barnum, Marg Williams, Shelley Andrews and Cindy Goehle for being such dear friends to me.

My Women's Business Group: Pat Herberger, Marcia Brogan, Mary Barber, Mari McNeil, Bonnie Roll, Jann MacDonald, Amy Jo Lauber, Paula Damico, Robin Lenhard and Paulette Krakowski. These women are brilliant, courageous and inspirations to everyone they meet.

To my sisters, Molly Gold, Amy Mullett and Susan Hannen, thank you for your love and beautiful souls.
To the Tannenhaus sisters, Judy, Jackie and Jill, my sincere thanks.

My sincere thanks to Lisa Coppola and Michele Pratt for their meticulous editing skills.

And once again, my thanks to Mary Dougherty, BootstrapPublishing.net and her talented staff for working so hard to make my blossom diaries a reality.

And most important of all, if it had not been for my dear friend and mother-in-law, Suzanne Marvin Flynn this series of blossom books never would have bloomed.

Introduction

There are no more precious possessions than memories nor any greater pleasures than the remembrance of past happiness. Yet Father Time, who throws an enchantment over remembered yesterday, is a bit of a thief too. He steals memories if you don't watch him. He is especially fond of stealing the little details that make memories vivid. How often have you, thinking back upon some happy day, been surprised to find you could not recollect it as clearly and completely as you would like? And how often have you been delighted when a friend, reminiscing with you about bygone times, has recalled to your mind some little detail of pleasure that you had completely forgotten?

A diary is a friend to go through life with you, sharing your thoughts and experiences, remembering them for you, and reminding you – years, perhaps, later – of all the pleasures great and small, that you have had together. It guards against the thievery of Father Time all the details that call back memories so vividly and brightly.

Start your diary then tonight. Put into it, as briefly as you choose a note of things you do, the friends who share your experiences, your work, your joys and sorrows. Let your diary be one of these friends to remember things for you. Then in future years you will have, whenever you wish, that rarest of pleasures – living over again the golden days that have gone by.

Prologue

When Deborah was born on April 18, 1920 her mother believed that her daughter was born with a broken heart. She did suffer from a newborn affliction, pyloric stenosis, which had absolutely nothing to do with the heart. However, Deborah's mother firmly believed that her baby was in need of a special amount of tender care. Mrs. Peters decided then and there that Deborah was to be her only child, and she would devote her life to guarding her daughter's heart.

She was my husband's Aunt Deborah and my dear mother-in-law, Laura's cousin. She was more like a sister to her as they grew up living close by, spending every holiday and special occasions together. When she passed, Laura lovingly handed over Deborah's leather-bound diaries to me. They are one of my most cherished gifts.

Deborah Elizabeth Peters had a rather long face, hauntingly penetrating blue eyes, a nose that took up a bit too much of her face and an enchanting smile. She believed herself to be quite beautiful. When she gazed in the mirror of her dressing table she saw a young woman who was every bit as beautiful as young Joan Crawford. She possessed an abundant amount of self-esteem. This, and her expertise at delivering the perfect kiss, made her quite desirable.

On December 25, 1936 Deborah saved the last, small, perfectly wrapped gift waiting for her under the Christmas tree. There were other lovely gifts from Mother and Dad: Evening in Paris perfume, lace underwear, a sea green satin housecoat, stunning evening slippers, Van Raalte silk stockings, red angora mittens, angora jacket, rhinestone bracelet, lilac satin nightgown, lamia blouse, Coty set, and a big surprise, a radio.

She waited until just before bed to open her last little gift. Deborah always loved to savor opening gifts. Mother and Dad had retired to their room after having spent the day reveling in their daughter's happiness. Mrs. Peters had left a gimlet glass chilling for Deborah in the icebox and a bit of champagne left for her to top off the day with.
The tree was all aglow, tinsel hung like shimmering icicles from nearly every branch and snow was dutifully falling in large white powder puffs framed by their lace curtains.

Deborah nestled in on their well-worn davenport, took a sip of champagne and carefully opened her last gift, a compact five-year diary of blue leather with a small gold blossom on the cover. A tiny gold key was taped on the back. Written inside the cover, in her mother's unmistakable flowing handwriting, was an inscription:

To my Darling Daughter,

A very Merry Christmas to you my dear. You will find that writing down your thoughts can be such a pleasure, such a joy. I have kept a diary for many years, and I can't imagine my life without one. It is true that a diary is a much trusted friend. With the turn of the tiny key your most private thoughts will be safe and sound. There is a magic to keeping a diary. Perhaps someday, many, many years from now your words will convey who you were and how you lived, and you will serve as an inspiration to another generation of women who share their thoughts, their loves, their memories with pen and ink.

Much love to you my daughter,

Mother

December 24, 1936

And so it began; Deborah's first diary.

Friday, January 1, 1937

The whole family felt very tired after the usual New Year's Eve celebration. Carol and Laura each were allowed a very small glass of champagne, no more than two sips. I thought since Carol is fifteen she should be allowed a full glass, but Mother said Laura might feel left out, and at twelve years of age more than two sips for Laura would not be prudent.

I made my scrapbook of King Edward, or rather, the Duke of Windsor. Margaret came over, and I drew some lovely pictures of Joan Crawford. Mother says I have Joan's features. I love the nail polish I got for Christmas; it's red like Mother's. Dad said it looks rather intense for a sixteen-year-old girl to wear, but Mother said it's perfectly all right.

Monday, January 4, 1937

We took the tree down today. What a dreadful sinking feeling I get when the fragrance of fir leaves the house. It's so very sad. I feel it right in the pit of my stomach. Mother says I'm like Camille swooning over a lost love. It is rather like a lost love, saying goodbye to Christmas.

Friday, January 29, 1937

We went to the station to meet Grandmother Peters this evening and I was the first to see her. I never was so glad to see a person in my life. I think she looks like the queen every time she steps off the train. She was dressed all in blue with a lovely thin veil draped down over her hat. How very elegant my grandmother is. Carol came with us too. I wish she and Laura were my sisters instead of my cousins. I don't really like being an only child. Dada is much more down to earth. Maybe it's because she lives off and on with us and we see her more often than

Grandmother Peters. I think it's wonderful that Dad doesn't mind Mother's mother living with us. It is a little strained when both grandmothers are in the house at the same time. I don't like it when Dada goes to live with Aunt Helen and Uncle Charlie. I miss her so. Grandmother Peters is grand for certain, but easier to take in small doses.

Sunday, January 31, 1937

My recital went off pretty good and I played rather well. Mother, Dad, Dada and Grandmother Peters were in the front row. I only hit one sour note and only Dad winced. I love taking them through the halls of Bennett. When we got home Mother made chocolate sodas for us, and Mrs. Brown brought over some homemade cookies to help us celebrate. She's a dear of a neighbor.

Monday, February 8, 1937

We are studying Shakespeare's sonnets in English class. They're terribly lovesick. I can tell that everyone in class is bored to death. How can they be so blind to love? I know love. I can honestly say that I am in love with Sullivan. Margaret says that we should get married in June. What a thought; married at seventeen. I would never consider getting married that young. I need to live before I get married.

Tuesday, February 16, 1937

Went to see *College Holiday* and *Back to Nature* with some of the kids and I practically had hysterics all through both of them! George Burns and Gracie Allen are so flawless with their humor. They never skip a beat. I love the fact that they are a real couple. Aunt Milly came with us. She was going to bring Carol and Laura, but she said they had too much homework to do. What a wonderful aunt she is. She was sweet and laughed right along with us. I love it when adults don't act like adults.

Friday, February 19, 1937

Had plenty of fun in English today. I said "Hi Sullivan" to a particular gent in the halls and he gave me a bit of a sly smile. Oh those Irishmen and their smiles. I think he's the nuts! He has blue eyes too and wavy black hair. Oh how beautiful our children would be. But the Irish like to have large broods of children. That's not for me.

This weather is so darn cold. I wish I had a project to focus on during these desolate months of winter. I want to learn how to knit. I always wanted to knit myself a sweater. I should start with a pair of socks or mittens first.

When I got home today I could feel a cold coming on. My throat was sore and I had such a chill. Mother put me right to bed and made me a hot toddy. I went to sleep with Sullivan whirling in my thoughts and big flakes of snow piling up on my window ledge, how snuggly.

Tuesday, February 23, 1937

Jimmie Fidler said on his program that Errol Flynn is going to be a war correspondent on the Spanish War for a British newspaper while in Europe. Errol is so brave, handsome and intelligent. I love his mustache. He occupies most of my thoughts.

Saturday, February 27, 1937

Margaret and I went to the movies all day today. We saw Fred MacMurray and Claudette Colbert in *Maid of Salem* and then to the *Hipp to see *Sea Devils* and *Career Woman*. There are so many times that I think I want to be a career woman. Of course that would mean no husband or children. That could never be for me. I want to be like Mother and Dad. Making a home is so important. I wish I could have both a career and a family, but I can't have it all. One or the other would have to suffer.

When we got home I couldn't stop talking about the movies. Mother had her hands over her ears begging me to not give the plots away.

April 19 and 20 will be Bennett's school play *The Ivory Door*. I'm so looking forward to seeing it.

Saturday, March 6, 1937

Errol was utterly terrific in *Green Light*. I sat through it twice of course! I just finished the most wonderful book, *I Am the Fox*. I have read half of it in one sitting. It's a great psychological story. The author is Winifred Van Etten – a feminist novelist.

Wednesday, March 10, 1937

I have just started *Gone With The Wind,* the much talked about best seller. I am so excited as I turn each page. I want it to last forever. Beautiful writing is such a treat to indulge in. I simply love reading a good book. I can't wait for the summer so I can ride my bike to the park and sit and read all afternoon. There are so many books and so little time to read them all. I'll have to choose carefully.

Sullivan kissed me today! It was quite by surprise I must say. Margaret and I were walking home from school and he ran up behind me, twirled me around and kissed me. It was at least three beats of a kiss; five beats is a movie kiss. Then he said "I bet Errol Flynn doesn't kiss that good." Then he laughed and ran down the street. It was just like in the movies! Margaret and I just looked at each other with astonishment.

* *Shea's Hippodrome Theatre was one of the movie palaces along Buffalo's Main Street. It stood approximately one block south of the Paramount Theater (previously Shea's Great Lakes Theater) and on the same side of the street.*

Thursday, March 18, 1937

I am trying to read *Gone With The Wind* as slowly as possible. I am savoring each word. It is the most perfect book I have ever read. I have fallen completely in love with the hero Rhett butler. He's devilish and romantic and quite scandalous. I would say, the perfect man.

I take the book wherever I go. Mr. Brewster got rather angry with me in Latin today, as I was trying to read a short passage while he wasn't looking. I got a little too engrossed and forgot to look up to keep an eye on him. Before I knew it he was standing next to me asking what Mr. Butler would think of our Latin class. I was told never to bring that book to class again.

Sunday, March 21, 1937

Finished *Gone With The Wind*! Oh how cruel Scarlett was to Rhett and then when she realized how she loved him, it was too late; the irony of fate. Read in the New York Times that Mr. Selznick has selected the cast for *Gone With The Wind*. Miriam Hopkins as Scarlett, Clark Gable as Rhett (thank God!) Leslie Howard as Ashley and Janet Gaynor as Melanie.

Today is the first day of spring. I do so love spring. It is the promise of warmth and blessings. I don't want to see anymore snow!

Sullivan asked me if I'd like to come over to his house to listen to his Benny Goodman records. I asked if his mother would be home. He made a funny face and said yes and that I would be safe. He hasn't actually asked me out. I find that rather perplexing since he gave me that kiss. Hmmm.

Saturday, March 27, 1937

I got a darling permanent today and went shopping with Mother. She bought me a new hat, bag and gloves in a lovely shade of blue. When I wear blue it always brings out the deep blue in my eyes.

I had fourteen girls over for the evening and midnight supper. We had chicken and potato salad. Mother made some crudités for us to munch on. We sang some great songs, *Don't Fence Me In, Pennies from Heaven, The Way You Look Tonight, When You Got a Good Friend,* and several more. Eight boys crashed and I had to feed the whole bunch. Mother said it was okay with her as long as the boys behaved like gentlemen. Thank goodness they did. Gee! Boy! What a party!

Wednesday, March 31, 1937

Ruth came over tonight. Mother and Dad were out. It's still snowing. I wish spring would come. Ruth and I talked about our future and what we want out of life. I haven't done that in a while. She simply can't wait to get married and settle down. She knows what her path in life is going to be. I don't feel that way. Of course there are times when I look at Sullivan and think how grand it would be to be married and live close to Mother and Dad.

Then there are times when I want more for myself. It's a little burning flame that I can't seem to extinguish. Not sure that I want that flame to go out. After Ruth left I stayed up until midnight listening to Benny Goodman's orchestra with all of the lights out, contemplating what life has in store for me.

Friday, April 2, 1937

Mother and I went to the Hipp to see Jean Harlow and Bob Taylor in *Personal Property*. What a scream! I simply love Jean Harlow. She's so beautiful and terribly funny. I know we would be friends if we were to meet.

Ruth had a party tonight. Sullivan was there but didn't seem to pay much attention to me. He was sitting with the guys most of the night. He's a mystery that one. I had on a very form-fitting sweater, and boy do I know he noticed. It seems like most of my clothes are in the color blue. I'll have to do some shopping and broaden my color choices.

Saturday, April 3, 1937

All us kids went to the Gamma Sig's dance. *Glen Gray and his Casa Loma Orchestra were too perfect. Afterwards we stopped at the Mayflower for drinks. I had my first *sidecar* cocktail. What a treat. I asked the bartender to write down the ingredients for me:

Sidecar drink – Created in Paris during WWI

- *1 1/2 ounces Cognac or Armagnac, or bourbon*
- *1 ounce Cointreau or triple sec orange liqueur*
- *1/2 ounce lemon juice*
- *Lemon twist for garnish*
- *Sugar for rimming (optional)*

I didn't get in until 4:45 a.m. I didn't feel tired though. I went for a long ride with Bill Sheldon. Smooth time. I've been trying to get a certain Irishman out of my thoughts.

There is a report that Errol Flynn has been killed on the Spanish war front. Please, this cannot be true. I will say prayers that he is spared.

*Glen Gray and his Casa Loma Orchestra was the first swing band. As early as 1929 they began playing the same mixture of hot jazz and sweet ballads that **Benny Goodman** would later popularize and that would dominate the music industry in the late 1930s and early 1940s.*

Monday, April 5, 1937

A bullet grazed Errol's temple, but he's all right now and is in Valencia, and he was seen at a bathing beach. The studio wants him home but he doesn't pay any attention. He is his own man. This is why I am drawn to him so. His beautiful looks have a little to do with it too.

A news flash concerning Errol: He has cabled his studio from Paris saying he has had enough excitement and will arrive on April 16th. We can all take a deep sigh of relief. I have been praying and praying for his safe return to us and the silver screen. What would Hollywood be without Errol Flynn!?

Wednesday, April 7, 1937

Turns out that Errol was never really shot. He was hit by a falling piece of plaster when the city was attacked. This was from his own lips.

I am fixing the attic room up swell. I love going up there and listening to the rain lightly tapping on the roof or thunderously pouring down. Mother doesn't know, but I have a candle that I light when I go up there. There is an overstuffed chair from Mother's old house that I have covered with Dada's quilt that she made for Mother when she got married. I have a little table with my candle on it in front of the oval window. It reminds me of looking out of a light house. I can see over the tree tops. I can think clearly when I'm up there.

I went to see Joan Crawford in The *Last of Mrs. Cheney*. She was perfect. I love the way she speaks. I wonder if she talks like that all the time. She's very deliberate with each word.

We have decided that I should go to New York with Mother and Dad next month. I know Mother wants to do some spring shopping. We have some lovely shops here in Buffalo, but nothing compares to the clothes that they have in New York. Just to see them in the store front windows is a thrill. We all enjoy taking in a show as well.

Sunday, April 18, 1937

My seventeenth birthday. Gee! I can't believe it! I got the *Green Light* novel, an *Evening in Paris* gift set, two pairs of silk stockings, one pair of socks, two bottles of sachet, dress material, a taffeta slip and a dollar. We had such a lovely dinner. Carol and Laura came over and we listened to records. I also read passages from *Gone With The Wind* to them. I love seeing how enthralled they become. Laura is only twelve, but she does seem to grasp the romantic aspect of the novel. Carol of course is much like myself and can immerse herself in the intensity of it all.

Wednesday, April 21, 1937

Errol is in trouble again. Knights of Columbus are investigating his activities in Spain. They charge that he and two other actors raised $1,500,000 for the Socialists in Spain. Flynn denies the charges. He's in New York. He certainly lives the life of an adventurer on screen and off. He is so fascinating, and I love to hear about everything that is going on in his life, although I'm sure that there is much about which his public is left in the dark. I can dream and imagine about what he's up to.

Went horseback riding with the gang today. Perfect day and such fun. Mitchell came over this evening. He tried to kiss me about ten times and I at last had to give in under his caveman tactics!

Thursday, April 29, 1937

Betty from next door came over and we listened to Bob Taylor and Irene Dunne in *Magnificent Obsession*. Bob Taylor is so attractive. I like him best with a mustache. I like to imagine him saying those romantic lines to me instead of his leading lady. When he has a close- up on the screen it's almost as though he's looking into my eyes.

I have finished *Green Light*. It was very uplifting.

I am up in my attic right now. The rain of April has arrived washing all of winter from our Buffalo neighborhoods. It's a tapping rain today. My candle is lit and my thoughts are whirling around my mind about my future once again. Who will I be? What lives will I touch? Will I be a wife and mother? Will I find grand and passionate love? Mother and Dad love each other. I know that, but passion? Passion seems to fade with marriage. I want to find a way to keep passion alive.

Does love creep up on you? Does it hit you like a bolt of lightning? I wonder. I have had boys kiss me and in that moment I was deeply in love with them. But then that intense love would fade until I was kissed again. How does love and passion hold on to your heart? How do people stay married to one person for their entire lives? I'm so young, I simply cannot imagine that kind of love, that kind of devotion. I know that it's wrong, but I found a touching letter from Dad to Mother written before they were married.

It was buried away in a hat box. I waited a very long time before I decided to read it. It's rather sad that Mother doesn't have it in a more cherished spot.

I would have never guessed that Dad could be so tender and loving to Mother. They seem to act more like very close cousins. I just never think of them as ever having been in love. At least not the kind of love that I think about and crave. I'm so pleased to know that they did feel that way at one point; at least Dad did.

Nov. 28, 1915

Dear Bess:
It was indeed kind of you to write me the sweet frank letter from Sag Harbor just previous to your return home.

Although seemingly preparing me for the worst, you allow me still to hope and in consequence my heart will continue to beat high with the greatest hope I will ever have.

You need never give a second thought to the fact that you are different from lots of girls. It is that same difference which is one of the many magnetic powers that drew me ever toward you. I hope also that I am different from a whole lot of men. If I did not think so I would never have the courage to ask you for the most priceless jewel you possess, namely yourself. I am glad you like the plant I bought for you. I trust it will thrive and grow, as your own womanly loveliness and my love for you is ever growing. I will try to be very patient and not worry you by any repetition of our lovely evening together, but it will be very difficult.

Please allow me to pay you the same little attentions that I have done in the past.

I was thinking not long ago of the first time I took you to the theatre about ten years ago. My first girl and still first in my thoughts. It reminds me of that beautiful book, "Their Yesterdays." I am praying daily that the ending will be the same – and with the ending great happiness for you and me.
As Ever Yours,
Bob

I do feel a slight twinge of guilt reading such a personal letter, but it is my family history and I would have come across it sooner or later. To read Dad's words of love to Mother fills my heart with hope for my own future. I think it's lovely how much Dad loved Mother. I hope with all my heart that someone loves me that much someday.

Ten years since their first date? That seems rather a long courtship. Mother certainly kept Dad waiting. I wonder if Dad has any love letters from Mother.

Saturday, May 1, 1937

Mother and Dad and I went to see *Green Light* for the third time. My heart was beating so fast just before it began. Mother could tell that I was flushed with excitement. She doesn't like it when I get too excited. She worries about my heart so.

Mother and Dad were crazy about the film and loved it. I could see that they both had tears in their eyes. Imagine!

I guess New York is off for now. Mother said that she thought the excitement of the city would be too much for me. I'm disappointed, but not devastated.

Bennett is going to have their annual speaking contest for Juniors May 14. I don't want to miss it.

Thursday, May 6, 1937

What tragedy! The Hindenburg burst into flames in the sky! Listening to it unfold on the radio is truly heartbreaking. What could possibly have happened? There were at least two hundred people on board. The images are too horrible to look at. You could hear the pain in the eyewitness reporter's voice as he described the explosion. I will pray for them tonight. What might those people have been thinking in their last moments?

It is tragedies like these that underscore my thoughts that you should live your life to the fullest and not acquiesce to rules and antiquated traditions. I want to make every single day count. Life is so very precious. People go through the motions day in and day out. They need to stop and appreciate the beauty that this one life has to offer. This tragedy has made me stop and think. This is indeed a very sad day.

Thursday, May 13, 1937

Yesterday was the coronation. I heard part of it over the air. Wally and Edward are going to be married soon. I still cannot believe how he gave up the thrown to be with the woman he loves. It is the most romantic thing I have ever heard of. Dad feels that it is shameful for him to turn his back on his country. Mother and I share the same thought, to love someone that much is simply magical.

My bedroom is all changed around and it looks swell.

Tonight was the Jr. Prom. I had a perfect time. I was cut in on three times during one dance. My dress was a beautiful shade of cornflower blue, again to match my eyes. Mother ordered a small bunch of flowers to match for my hair. I dabbed some Evening in Paris on and I was off for the night. John Darnell was my escort for the evening. I could see Sullivan in the corner watching us dance. He had his chance.

Monday, May 17, 1937

Dad got home today. We certainly did miss him. He said he almost missed the train. It rained all day. There is no furnace fire going so we have to light the fireplace. Dad brought in a big load of wood and said it was good to get the chill out of the air. We all snuggled in and listened to Lux Radio Theater. I took a long hot bath then went to bed.

Wednesday, May 19, 1937

Today is Mother's birthday. After school I came home and got my homework done. We are going to have such fun tonight. We went to the Statler for dinner, how devastatingly beautiful Mother looked. She wore a lovely dress in lavender with matching shoes and bag. We both love "Evening in Paris." I love this scent because it will always remind me of my mother. Whenever I catch that fragrance I will think of my mother.

After dinner we went to Shea's Buffalo to see Horace Heidt's Orchestra. It was a swell show. I couldn't stay still in my seat the music was so grand. Dad has real respect for Horace Heidt because of Heidt's motto: "It's better to build boys than to mend men."

Friday, May 21, 1937

Ruth, Margaret and I took the Olds out to the Park Club. We each had a sidecar and Margaret put it on her father's club bill. How decadent it feels to do something like that. She simply signed for them. It was as though money had no real significance. Oh to be wealthy.

I had to sit in the rumble seat and got caught in the rain on the ride home. I was simply drenched. I had a chill that just wouldn't go away so I took another long bath and got in bed with a good book and a hot toddy.

I have a pile of books next to my bed that I can't wait to read. Ruth wants to borrow *Camille,* but it's my favorite book. I know she would return it, but it's one of my closest friends. Books mean that much to me.

I read for hours before I fell asleep. I love having my window open so I can hear the rain. My room is such a sanctuary for me. It's all mine and I have it just the way I want it. I do feel sorry for other girls who have to share a room with a sister.

Wednesday, May 26, 1937

Went to see *A Star is Born* with Janet Gaynor and Frederick March. What a heartwarming picture and oh! Freddie! Can he kiss. He's drunk in it most of the time, but oh! Oh! Oh! does he spell sex-appeal!

Janet was sweet in the role, but I feel that someone more beautiful should have played that character. Janet's voice is so squeaky at times. I think Joan Crawford would have done a much better job.

I think I'll see if Carol and Laura would like to see it with me.

Sunday, May 30, Memorial Day 1937

We all took a ride out to Olcott Beach. Ruth came with us and we brought our roller skates. I do love it out here. Lake Ontario is so beautiful. I love laying on the beach and soaking up the sun.

Mrs. Little came over and said that she heard on the radio that if the British get in the war Errol Flynn will leave the movies.

Thursday, June 3, 1937

Edward and Wally were married this morning by an Episcopal Minister who defied the Church of England. Hooray! What a very brave man. I'm sure that the entire country is very upset with him for having chosen love over the church.

I adore the simple elegant white suit that she wore. She knows just how to present herself. You can tell how very much in love they are. I say bravo to both of them! They deserve their happiness. Here's to a long life of happiness for the Duke & Duchess!

Monday, June 7, 1937

Gorgeous Jean Harlow died today, a victim of uremic poisoning. I listened to Errol Flynn on Lux Theatre and De Mille was so broken up over Harlow that he could hardly speak. His tribute at the end of the program was wonderful. I can't seem to stop crying over this tragic loss.

William Powell and her mother, Mrs. Bello, were with her to the end. After her death Powell rushed out of the room to Warner Baxter who was in the hall and exclaimed, "My God Warner, she's dead!"

Jimmy Fidler's tribute to Jean was so touching: "Her heart was more beautiful than her platinum hair. Wherever you are I hope you're tuned in to this program dear girl. So long Jean; we loved you. Good night."

Such a loss. She was only twenty-six. We all have to live life to the fullest.

Wednesday, June 9, 1937

Saw Clark Gable and Myrna Loy in *Parnell*, beautifully done. I wish I could have kept my mind on the movie. The News Reel was filled with touching tributes to Jean Harlow.

Jean Harlow's funeral was today. It was a Christian Science service. The casket was banked with lilies of the valley and gardenias. Clark Gable was one of the pallbearers. William Powell is obviously heartbroken. I do believe that he would have married her. They didn't care at all about the difference in their age. Age simply does not matter. When you love someone love is the only thing you should be at all concerned about. What does a few years matter?

Saturday, June 12, 1937

Mother and I went downtown for lunch at the Top O 'The Town. No cocktails as it was too early. We went shopping afterwards and I got a bathing suit, turban (white), shoes, panties, silk stockings and some new stationery. I'm all set for summer.

Margaret and I went to see Robert Montgomery in *Night Must Fall*. It was weird as heck, and he had a twisted mind in it. Smooth acting though. His character was so strange. He was a very handsome and likeable fellow, but yet he had a woman's head in a hatbox under his bed.

We drove out to Park Club with a few of the kids.

Wednesday, June 30, 1937

Mother and I went downtown today. Had lunch at the Top O' The Town Restaurant. It was a late lunch, around 2:30. Mother said that it would be perfectly all right for us to have a cocktail with lunch. She had a daiquiri and I had a sidecar. I sipped mine very slowly as to enjoy the entire experience.

I love Mother so. She is truly an elegant woman. I wanted to talk to her about boys and what to expect when they become men. When I touched on the subject she quickly moved onto how fun my trip will be with Ruth.

There was a very handsome man sitting at the table next to us. He kept looking over and smiling at me. I believe he was in his mid to late forties. Way too old for me. It doesn't really matter though. He was sitting with his wife.

Friday, July 2, 1937

Ruth and I took the bus from Buffalo to Albany. Smooth trip, bus filled with interesting fellows. Two of them taxied with us to our hotel and paid the fare. We quickly thanked them and made a beeline for our room. The Hotel Leneyck is just lovely. We stayed the night, rather uneventful, and almost missed our bus to Lake Champlain. How gorgeous it is here. Miss Severence's house is lovely. We spoke French at the supper table. I still have to pinch myself. Having our French teacher invite us to her summer home to improve our speaking skills is beyond exciting.

Our room is beautiful, very bohemian! It's decorated in lush colors of lavender and gold. It speaks of France, and there is a fragrance of another time which I cannot place.

Sunday, July 4, 1937

We went swimming twice. Lots of fire crackers were going off and sparklers were lighting up the beach. At the end of the day we had a weiner roast on the shore. How beautiful the sunset was; a great orange ball sitting in the sky. Since it was such an intimate setting I decided to be quite bold and ask Miss Severence the question I asked Mother at lunch. Ruth had gone to bed and it was just the two of us by the fire. I asked her what to expect from men, what they will want from us as women, aside from the obvious.

She became rather pensive. I was so pleased that she didn't dismiss me. She looked beyond me and was staring intent on the lake. She spoke quietly to me in French. She spoke without hesitation, not looking at me once.

"When boys become men they decide whether they will become men of integrity or bags of appetites to be filled. Those who seek integrity are easy to love, the appetite-seekers are clever and are never satisfied. We women have to decide what our preference will be, and if we'll be able to live with our choice."

She then turned to me and put her hand on mine and smiled. I have lived by those words. I will never forget how her eyes misted over. It was a tender moment between the two of us.

Wednesday, July 7, 1937

I got an unexpected postcard from my friend Shelley, and I wrote an eleven-page letter to Mother. We are reading old French legends and they are very interesting. I had a ride in a truck down to the beach. I wrote a letter to Norma Shearer. Wouldn't it be wonderful if she wrote me back? She is one of my favorite actresses.

I went swimming nude in the lake. What a delicious feeling. I had plenty of pictures snapped of me in the nude while swimming. There were a group of fellows from the village up on the shore hiding behind trees. Not very well though. The human body is nothing to be ashamed of. It's the boys who should be ashamed of themselves. Later in the evening they climbed up a ladder to our sleeping porch. Did we have fun!

Saturday, July 10. 1937

I got a letter from Mother. She misses me so. We met the fellows again over at the store. The cutest one is Harold Ero, part Indian and one of thirteen. He's a very good kisser I must say. I went to his baseball game, he's very good with a bat. Harold has very dark thick hair with dark brown eyes. I believe he's over six feet tall. He has this wonderful scent of pine with a touch of camp fire about him. It's a clean smell, very enticing.

One of the girls who lives in the village said that the town thinks Ruth and I are scandalous. I'm sure she sees us as some kind of threat. It is thrilling what! Ruth and I went canoeing this evening. It was gorgeous. The moon was so big and silvery across the lake.

Tuesday, July 13, 1937

Went on a two-day hiking trip with Miss Severence, her niece Lucy, who just arrived and Ruth of course. We slept out of doors on the hard ground and boy was it cold. We kept a fire burning all night. It was some experience.

We went through Lost River Gorge. What fun we had scrambling through rocks underground and what a cute guide we had. His name is Mike and I'd say he's around 21 or so. I guess the whole town knew That we went away for two days with a male guide. I'm not going to let their narrow minds bother me. I'll never forget the history of Lost River Gorge. Mike told it so well.

I'm going to write down what the brochure said so I will be able to tell my children all about it:

"The Lost River Gorge & Boulder Caves, located in New Hampshire's Kinsman Notch in the White Mountains, is a land of spectacular beauty forged by the powerful forces of water, wind, weather, and time. The shaping of Kinsman Notch and the surrounding mountains began about 300 million years ago. The Ice Age brought glaciers more than a mile thick that grounded, lifted, and deposited rocks that formed notches and mountains. When the ice melted, the

water carried debris, eroding the rocks and forming Lost River Gorge.Lost River is so-named because the brook draining from the south east part of Kinsman Notch disappears below the surface in the narrow, steep-walled glacial gorge. The Gorge is partially filled with immense blocks of granite, through which the brook cascades along its subterranean course until it eventually emerges and joins the Pemigewasset River, which flows south from Franconia Notch.The first documented exploration of Lost River took place in 1852. Similar to Alice's tumble down the rabbit hole in *Alice in Wonderland*, local historian Elmer E. Woodbury wrote about how the Jackman brothers, Royal and Lyman, were fishing along the stream. The boys worked their way over and around the boulders when suddenly Lyman disappeared out of sight as if the earth had swallowed him. Lyman had slipped into a moss covered hole and fallen into a cave about 15 feet below into a pool of water about waist deep. Now known as *Shadow Cave*, it was the first of the many caves the boys would soon discover. In the early 1900s, as logging increased in the area and threatened the beauty of Lost River Gorge and the surrounding area, there was a need to protect this natural wonder. A newly formed, private non-profit conservation organization – The Society for the Protection of New Hampshire Forests recognized that need and purchased Lost River in 1912. Still owned by the Forest Society today, and now leased and operated by the White Mountains Attractions Association, the two organizations work closely together to provide guests the opportunity to experience the fun, challenge, and excitement of Lost River – just as the Jackman Brothers did over 150 years ago."

Thursday July 15, 1937

We helped Miss Severence clean the house. I was in charge of the carpet sweeping and Ruth dusted the furniture. All of the windows were open and we were blessed with a soft breeze filling the house as we worked. Miss Severence ironed the linens and we all sat at the dining room table cleaning the silver. There was a sweeping "S" on each piece. Then she made a large pitcher of lemonade. Delicious! This evening we went to bed early. We were so tired. Catch-up sleep was called for. It was not to be. All the fellows rode back and forth on their bicycles singing "Buffalo gals, are ya comin' out tonight?" Boohoo! They were clinking beer bottles too. We thought it best to stay put. Miss Severence heard the commotion and shooed the boys away. We couldn't contain ourselves. Ruth and I couldn't stop giggling. We had a hard time falling to sleep wondering how far they had been shooed away. I finally drifted off with the tune of all those boys singing to us Buffalo Gals whirling in my dreams.

Tuesday, July 20, 1937

Went to the library today and got some books. It rained like hell today. We all listened to Stanley Pike play his banjo on the hotel porch. I'm having such a grand time here. We are considered "City Girls" and everyone thinks we are quite experienced women.

Sunday, July 25, 1937

We all went to the ball game. Isle La Motte won 6-0. The crack of the bat is such a sound of summer. Ruth and I brought a wool blanket and laid it out in the shade of several enormous oak trees. Miss Severence made some lemonade for us and I brought some cookies mother had sent me.

Harold is quite the athlete. He scored a home run hitting the ball so far it went into the woods and they couldn't find it. Luckily they had another ball. After the game the boys followed us down the road. They took us to an old barn where they want to have a barn dance. It was so hot we went down by the water and jumped in. How refreshing! What fun! It's just like one of those Bing Crosby movies. I love it here!

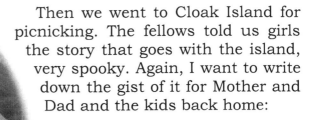

Then we went to Cloak Island for picnicking. The fellows told us girls the story that goes with the island, very spooky. Again, I want to write down the gist of it for Mother and Dad and the kids back home:

"Off of Isle La Motte's south east coast is a small island with a weird name, Cloak Island. Why would you name an island Cloak Island? As the story goes, a domestic quarrel in the 1770s boiled over when Eleanor Fisk got sick on her husband's angry temper. She hitched up her team of horses and set out across the frozen lake towards Alburgh, but never made it. Later, her red cloak was found along the bushes and rocks of the island, which would forever be known as Cloak Island.

There is another variation of the story. After Eleanor Fisk went missing, concerned townsfolk suspected she had drowned but needed proof. So, they gathered down near the lake and dropped her red cloak into the water. An old Yankee superstition dictated that to find the body of a drowned victim all you had to do was drop a cloak belonging to the missing woman in the water and it will come to rest above the body. The cloak eventually found its way over to the island and got tangled on the beach, thus giving Isle La Motte's tiny neighbor its name." I do love a good ghost story.

Tuesday, July 27, 1937

I went walking with Harold down by the water. There is something so romantic about sitting by a lake or a river with a handsome young man. It's fun to imagine what my life would be like if I stayed here and married Harold. I certainly wouldn't want to have 13 children, that's for certain. It is beautiful and peaceful and quiet here. However, I'm sure the winters are no fun.

We decided to tell Miss Severence about the fellows. She said it was all right to go walking with them but not to get in cars. Well we did get in a car tonight and had piles of fun! What the hell!

We all decided to go to the graveyard. All of these souls buried here for eternity. It kind of makes you want to live for the moment. We really do only have such a short time to make hay while the sun shines. There was a beautiful full moon shinning up in the dark sky. We found a spot by a big old tree and started necking. Oh that Harold!

Friday, July 30, 1937

Oh my heart! Today is our last day. Miss Severence hosted a small party for us and even provided a bottle of white wine that was served with dinner. We had chicken with a sweet French sauce and slices of tomatoes in a lovely dressing. Miss Severence brought out her fine china and her lace linens. I was very nervous as the sauce had a red hue to it and I didn't want to transfer it to her lovely linens.

Of course Harold came over to say good-bye. Tonight he smelled of soap, not a flowery soap, just a very fresh clean smell. He wore a tie, which I thought was sweet. We went out on the lake in his family's canoe. There was a tinge of cool air about us, but I was all warm inside. He said that he would write to me. I do so hope that he follows through.

When we got back to shore he asked me to take a walk with him back to the graveyard. He had a blanket and a basket waiting for us. There were two beers and a sandwich for us to share. We drank the beers and skipped the sandwich. He kissed me about 20 times. This is the furthest I have gone with any other boy.

Oh how wonderful it is to be young in the summer. I haven't a care in the world and I've made some grand new friends. Everything is so new and fun when you are only 17. I love this age.

Walking back, I had the most wonderful feeling of being completely and totally content. This is such a wonderful summer.

Monday, August 16, 1937

I haven't had a moment to write in my diary since I got back from New Hampshire. I was in such a state missing the fellows and of course Harold in particular. Oh that dark, dark hair and those luscious lips. It has been over two weeks and I haven't received a letter from him yet.

There are boys here of course that I have been neglecting. I do hope that out of sight doesn't truly mean out of mind with Harold. I do have to remember that I have options.

Wednesday, August 25, 1937

Got a letter from Harold this morning. I was plenty excited until I actually read it. He writes awful and misspells a lot of words. Intelligence means just as much to me as a handsome face and athletic body. He wants my picture and says he'll send me one of him later. He also writes that he and some of the fellows are planning a trip to come and see us. It would be nice to see him again. Does absence make the heart grow fonder, or out of sight out of mind? Hmmm.

Sunday, August 29, 1937

I felt rather "off" today. Sunday is always an uninteresting day anyway. I got to day dreaming about Isle La Matte and that always makes me feel lonely. I miss how independent I felt when I was there. I could smoke with my legs up on the chez lounge on the screened in porch. I'd sip my ice-tea and listen to the sounds of the forest. Miss Severence treated me as an adult, not a silly school girl. I miss that so.

Monday, August 30, 1937

I listened to the Louis–Farr fight. They battled for 15 rounds, Farr making a wonderful showing but Louis retained the championship. It was the best fight I ever heard. Not many women like to listen to fights, but my heart races when I think about those two strong specimens duking it out!

Took a cool bath and put some of Mother's bath salts in the water. It felt so relaxing and gave me a nice boost of energy. Heat certainly can sap you.

I'm starting *The Professor's House* by Willa Cather tonight. I love her writing.

Saturday, September 4, 1937

Saw Sonja Henie and Tyrone Power in *Thin Ice*. Simply the best! Tyrone Power is what I would call a beautiful man. I prefer the more rugged type. While I was gone Don Robinson came over to see me twice in his Packard car. Wow! Wonder what he has on his mind? I'd love to have taken a ride with him, but I'm thinking it was probably best that I wasn't home. I don't want him to think that I'll always be available.

Watching Sonja on the screen made me wonder what I would look like as a blonde. I might like to try that some time.

Tuesday, September 7, 1937

My friend Jane Outerson is back in town. She, Chuck, Mitchell and I went for a ride in Mitch's car. The guys took us to see the "Purple Light" so-called house of prostitution in Buffalo. If Mother ever knew she'd kill me! We did see a car on a side street just sitting there, and then a man in a grey fedora stepped out, looked up and down the street and then went into the house. So very intriguing!

Friday, September 10, 1937

Mitchell and Chuck came over today, and we played some bridge. They are a perfect pair of nuts! I doubt their sanity most of the time. They both have very good physiques though! Chuck is so funny. He always makes me laugh. That's on my list. If I'm going to go steady with a boy he has to have a great sense of humor, not a clown of course.

I have to get my ice skates sharpened. Sonja Henie in *Thin Ice* reminded me to get ready for winter fun.

Saturday, September 11, 1937

I saw *Dead End*. It was too absorbing for words. The six boys from the original stage play made the picture. In my opinion, Humphrey Bogart was matchless as the gangster. They all had such grit to them. I have to wonder if they are like that in real life. It's hard to believe they could be anything but what they portrayed on the screen. Realism at its best!

Friday, September 17, 1937

I heard a rumor today that Mitchell will be a father one of these days, some girl who is a maid over in Canada. I find it hard to believe. Anyway I'm going to keep my mouth shut about it. Rumors can be a terrible thing. I do so hope that it's a rumor. He's way too young to be a father. I hope he's more careful from now on.

I'm going to take a nice long bath and lay on my bed and read for a while. Not sure what I'll be up to tonight.

I'm loving *The Professor's House*. I want it to last, so I'm reading it slowly. Tom, the main character, seems like just the type of young man I could go for.

Monday, September 20, 1937

I got a letter from Don at Duke University today, and he wants me to write to him, oh boy! This is hot stuff! He is so handsome! I am literally walking on air. I took cousin Carol and little cousin Laura to see *Dead End* again. I think Laura was a little frightened. Bogart is a very large presence on the screen. I was just as thrilled the second time around. Oh! Those *Dead End* kids! They are so tough, but that's what I like; Billy Halop especially.

Friday, September 24, 1937

Mother was playing the piano when I got home from school today. What a lovely way to be greeted at the end of the day. I sat down next to her on the piano bench and put my arm around her and gave her a hug. I don't know of any of my friends who have such a loving relationship with their mothers. Mine is rare indeed.

I went dancing with my friend Tommy; he's such a sweet and quiet boy. He sits at the table as my escort and other boys come over and ask me to dance. It never seems to bother him. What a relief! I'm not really attracted to him in that way, but I do like him as a friend.

He's going to go to school in Washington, and he wants me to visit him. I doubt Mother and Dad will let me go any time soon. It would be so thrilling to be in that exciting city with all of the political intrigue going on. I bet I will be able to visit him next year. I could try to get Mother and Dad to understand the educational aspects of the trip. Anyway, Tommy isn't the lover boy type.

I do want to go on an exciting adventure. I know Mother and Dad will relent.

Sunday, September 26, 1937

I went to church and Sunday school. What a beautiful fall day it is. I love every season. Each one comes with a gift all of its own. I do wish winter could be a little shorter. I could smell the smoke from our fireplace all the way down the street. Mother starts fires as soon as there is a slight chill in the air. Dad says we go through too much wood because of it. I'm with Mother on this one.

When I came in the door she asked me to sit with her by the fire. We had a quick cocktail before Dad got home.

Chuck and Mitchell came over dressed to kill. They were rare as usual. I kissed them both good night or rather it was the other way around.

Friday, October 1, 1937

More fun in school! Met Bob Sullivan in the hall today. He still likes to tease me. I'm never quite sure what he's thinking.

I went dancing at the Glen Park Casino with Tommy and a bunch of kids. What fun! Life is grand! There was a bit of a chill in the air so I decided to wear my red sweater. I'm so glad that I did. It became much cooler as the night went on. We all had such a grand time. The music drifted out from the casino and couples were dancing under the stars. What a beautiful night it was.

Saturday, October 2, 1937

Had to do some shopping today. I went downtown and bought a stunning gray coat military style, trimmed with gray Persian lamb. I also got a pair of black suede pumps and new stockings. It was just about five o'clock by the time I was finished and I thought I would slip into the Lafayette Hotel for a sidecar. Oh how my feet were killing me. I spotted a small table in the corner and made a beeline for it. I slipped my shoes off under the table so no one could see. I piled my bags on the chair next to me in case some young man might get ideas as to try and join me. I sipped it so slowly as to enjoy every drop thoroughly. And I did.

Friday, October 8, 1937

Chuck was hit by a truck! He got hit on the head and has a dislocated jaw. The car was wrecked badly. I'm so glad that it wasn't any more serious than that. I think he should have gone to the hospital. The doctor came to his house, but I would think x-rays would be in order.

I got a letter from Don today! It was a riot. He and another guy went beering and ended up with corn whiskey. He felt lousy the next day. According to custom he ended the letter "Soberly yours."

Sunday, October 10, 1937

Mitchell came over this evening. He kissed me goodnight about ten times. Boy! What technique! He's a nice boy, but I'm not crazy about him. He is funny. You have to love a man who can make you laugh, but there has to be something more. I do think Chuck is funnier, more natural at it.

Tuesday, October 12, 1937

Chuck was over this afternoon and then in the evening. He took me down to Parkside for a soda. I couldn't help myself. I ordered a hot fudge sundae with all of the extras. I deserve to treat myself with a few extra calories from time to time. Then we went for a long walk. I love taking walks on October nights. There is that crunchy smell of leaves beneath your feet and the air is cool, and crisp, but not cold. Mother and Dad weren't home when we got back to the house. Boy can Chuck neck! I can still feel those soul kisses.

Saturday, October 16, 1937.

I went to Miss Severence's for tea. Ever since the summer I feel that we have a true bond as women. Of course we could never be friends while I am still in school, but I do see us becoming closer when I get older.

Her apartment is much like I expected it to be, rather continental. She likes deep colors and soft lighting. How French she is!

I went to Bennett's football game. They were beaten 7-0 by East. What a letdown! Chuck came over after the game to help me with my homework. He did some other work too. Chuck says that if you think necking and petting is all right, then do it and don't give a damn what others think!

Wednesday, October 20, 1937

I had loads of home-work. Sometimes I catch myself day dreaming in history class over Don or Chuck. My, what a dilemma I'm in. Any way you look at it, its love!

The one thing about Chuck is that he's close by. Don is so far away at school. You know what they say; a bird in the hand is worth two in the bush.

I found a letter waiting for me on the dining room table when I came down stairs. It was a letter from Don. He wrote me on the day he got my last letter. I think he's very considerate and oh, those eyes!

Saturday, October 23, 1937

I feel as though I have been spending a great deal of time with the boys and neglecting my girlfriends. I called Ruth and Margaret up and asked if they'd like to sleep over. They agreed and we made our plans.

Mother made us a batch of her amazing Manhattans and oh, were they good! We stayed up until well after 1:00 a.m. talking about, what else, Boys!

Friday, October 29, 1937

Saw Ronald Coleman in *Prisoner of Zenda*. What intense love scenes! You can almost feel Ronald Coleman's arms around you pulling you closer to him for a deep kiss.

I went to a school dance with Dick Gedney and the gang. I had a hot roast beef sandwich and two Bacardi cocktails afterward at Coles. He looked so handsome tonight. He had on a blue sweater. I know his mother knit it for him. She has such talent. And it was the dreamiest shade of blue, almost like the lake.

Autumn seems to be turning into winter rather quickly.

Saturday, October 30, 1937

I attended Dick Gedney's party, and he had a scavenger hunt. I learned part of the "Big Apple." I just love to dance.

Janice Watson, a girl from my French class, and her boyfriend crashed the party, but Dick didn't mind. We all went driving and visited seven different places ending up at the Waldorf Lunch Box. I got home at 4:30 a.m. I'll never forget tonight. Gee! It was the nuts! Flaming youth! May it be like this forever! I haven't received a letter from Don in a while. I hope he's still thinking of me.

I feel like sleeping in all day tomorrow. I'm falling into bed as I write this.

Tuesday, November 2, 1937

Today is "All Souls Day," the day when the veil is the thinnest between this world and the next. I believe when my time comes I will visit the people I have loved. My loved ones will know that it's me with the unseasonable scent of lilacs, a soft warm breeze on a cold day and the chiming of church bells in the distance. The scent, the touch and the sound will allow them to think of me. I must remember to write this down and leave it for my children so they will know.

Not many 17-year-old girls think this way. Mother says that I am an old soul. I tend to agree. I'm quite certain I have lived many lives. I know that I have lived in England. I have such love for the country and its people. It's not only that, I truly feel that I was an English girl living in a grand castle.

I suddenly had the oddest chill.

Saturday, November 20, 1937

Nothing much at all has happened to me this month, with the exception of having the flu for two weeks. I simply felt awful. Mother took such good care of me, and the doctor came over twice. I didn't feel that it was necessary, neither did Dad, but Mother is always so worried about my heart. I don't know why. I'm as sound as a bell. I'm feeling fit as a fiddle now. Chuck was over this afternoon. We had quit a strenuous work-out. He may not have the charm I'm looking for in a man, but he definitely has a skill worth applauding. He is a handsome boy, and strong. His kisses aren't overpowering, but gentle and quite welcome.

It snowed today so we made a fire. Chuck brought four loads of wood in for Mother, and boy did she appreciate it. She said she would make him an apple pie for his efforts. I'm an expert at building a fire, just the right stacking technique. The aroma of baked apples coming from the kitchen was intoxicating. Chuck couldn't wait until he got home to have a piece. He sat right down at the kitchen table with a big pitcher of milk and ate half the pie.

I'm glad that Mother made a pie for us as well.

Friday, December 3, 1937

I went Christmas shopping with the girls. We went downtown and decided to try to get as much shopping done as possible. I bought a lovely handbag for Mother and I bought handkerchiefs for her as well. I ended up buying a dress and a slip for myself. Ruth and Bee made out better than I did as far as making a dent in their shopping list.

We went to the Statler for a cocktail and ended up having two. How elegant it all was. We of course didn't sit at the bar but at a booth with a dreamy light on the table. I felt a bit like Joan Crawford sitting there with my lovely friends. We had to make a point of it not to giggle and be immature. When we left there was a light snow coming down. It really got us in the spirit of the holidays.

Ruth asked us if we would like to go to the Saturn Club as her guests for dinner some night before Christmas. Ruth's family has gobs of money, but it was still so kind of her to ask. She said that the club is just stunning for the holidays. Ruth has always been very kind and generous. Some day she said she'll have her wedding at the club. I know it will be a grand one with all of the trimmings.

Christmas is in the air!

Wednesday, December 15, 1937

Dinner with Bee at Ruth's club! When she said it was stunning during the holidays she wasn't exaggerating one bit. There were Christmas trees in every room. As you walked down the great hall it was all decked out in swags of evergreens with big red bows. It was reminiscent of an English castle fit for a king and queen. I'm so glad that I wore my red velvet and black pumps. I fit right in with all of the holiday decorations. Ruth's father took a picture of all the girls next to the largest Christmas tree in the Red Room. The rich scent of pine simply filled the club.

We started off with sidecars. Dave the bartender makes the very best according to Ruth. He was so kind to us. We were told we could order whatever we wanted and I decided to get the duck. Oh, it was simply devastating. There were Christmas carolers walking through the club entertaining us all. We had candles on our table in silver candle sticks. The room was filled with friends and families laughing and filled with excitement. I do so love Christmas!

Friday, December 24, 1937

Christmas Eve – the night of nights! We went to church at 11:00 p.m. It was so beautiful and warm. I felt so spiritual and I tried to meditate on all that I am grateful for. Mother and Dad are such a blessing to me. I hope that I express that to them enough.

I love the way church smells at Christmas, all filled with pine, perfume and incense.

When we got home I stood looking at the tree tonight with all of the presents beneath it. I truly believe that there is something that we cannot touch or see, something that makes life worth living and working hard for. Christmas is that time of year where you look back and think of all of the wonderful treasures you have in life. Treasures you cannot hold in your hand but in your heart. Mother, Dad and Dada certainly fit into that gift. That magic spell is all around me; I am blessed.

I write these words just before I go to bed. I'm going to leave my door open tonight to allow the sweet scent of pine to drift up the stairs. I will put my head on my pillow and snuggle in and say my prayers for love, kindness and peace for everyone I know and hold dear. Amen.

Saturday, December 25, 1937

I got entirely too much for Christmas! The perks of being an only child I suppose. I was so pleased that Mother liked her bag and handkerchiefs. Dad was thrilled with the tie and cologne I got him.

We went over to Uncle George and Aunt Milly's for dinner. Carol and Laura were so darling. They loved showing me all of their gifts. We gave them each their own vanity set. Laura sat by the tree looking in her mirror and brushing her hair. I'm so pleased that they liked their sets. I chose a light pink set for Carol and a lavender set for Laura.

Oh how I ate! And the wine made the food even better. The French say that wine with dinner is a must. It brings out the flavor of each bite.

Friday, December 31, 1937

I dressed and took great care so I would look my very best for Chuck tonight. I was so thrilled that he had asked me to be his date on New Year's Eve. He said that the evening would start with cocktails at Mann's and we would have dinner at Laube's Old Spain, that he had dinner reservations at 8:00 p.m. He was to pick me up promptly at 6:30 p.m.

I waited around for Chuck all evening! At a quarter to ten he called quite plastered and said that he'd be over in twenty minutes to pick me up. I said, "No thank you!" and hung up. Mother and Dad were very upset for me, but I rallied and stayed up with them to usher the New Year in. I wasn't going to let Chuck ruin their evening.

I don't really like New Year's Eve anyway.

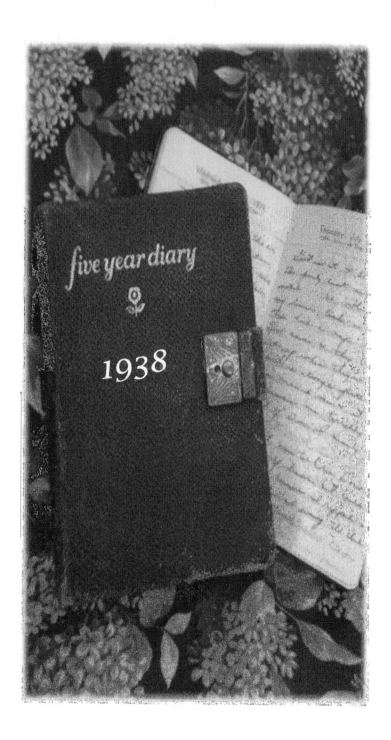

Saturday, January 1, 1938

I sat around all morning sulking over having been stood up. Mother made me some of her famous cinnamon rolls and coffee. I sat by the fire and looked at all of my lovely gifts. I should take them up to my room, but I enjoy having them displayed under the tree. We'll be taking it down tomorrow.

In the afternoon of all surprises I couldn't believe who showed up. It was Chuck, hat in hand, feeling terrible over his actions. He apologized to me and then to Mother and Dad. Dad wasn't as forgiving, but Mother said that boys will be boys and gave him some leftover Christmas cookies.

His excuse was that he had saved up for a very special evening for the two of us and that he had to lend the money to someone, but he couldn't tell me who it was. Sadly, I believe I know who he gave the money to. I know his father lost his job just before Christmas. I wish he had told me. We could have enjoyed a lovely night at home.

Friday, January 7, 1938

Chuck was over this afternoon. He's so strong! Wow! He stretched out on the floor and let me jump on his stomach to prove just how strong he is. No other movie stars thrill me any more with his technique. He stayed until 5:30 p.m. We did a lot of heavy petting and boy; does it get me hot. I have to take a deep breath and know just when to stop. It isn't easy.

Mother and Dad were out for the evening. Dad's expression on his face when he saw that Chuck was over was anything but pleasant. Chuck left shortly after they got home.

I think I'm going to take a long walk tomorrow. Nice crisp, clean air will help me to clear my mind. I have so much to think about; you do when you're this age.

Wednesday, January 19, 1938

Don came over today. He braved the storm for me. I certainly was glad that we didn't take down the mistletoe because when he saw it hanging over his head he gave me a big kiss. Shortly thereafter Dad pulled it down.

It snowed a great deal today. Don was such a dear and did the shoveling for Dad. He digs right into those piles of snow and shovels as though it is no effort at all. He's like a machine.

Thursday, February 3, 1938

Benny Goodman is at the 174th Armory tonight! I'm going with the girls and are we excited. I just love that swing music. I can't sit still. I just have to dance!

I was thinking about Chuck when I was sitting at my vanity table combing my hair. The doorbell rang and it was he. He's such a darling. We played bridge with Mother and Dad for a while. I asked him if he was going to see Benny Goodman tonight and he said he didn't have the money for a ticket. I wish he had thought ahead and saved up. I know his father found a job, so his money is his own now.

Saturday, March 5, 1938

I haven't had a minute to write in my diary all month. It's such a dark and dreary month. At least we are out of February. I'm making up for not keeping up with my diary today. As I look out my bedroom window I can see the sun beginning to peek out through the trees. March usually comes in like a lion and out like a lamb. I hope we have more lamb-like weather.

Summer will be here before we know it. But as Mother always tells me, don't wish your life away.

I saw *Snow White and the Seven Dwarfs*! It was marvelously done. What beautiful and vivid colors! Snow White had the most darling voice. I do so hope my Prince Charming will come someday soon.

I was over to see Carol today to tell her about *Snow White and the Seven Dwarfs*, when I bumped into Chuck. He walked me the rest of the way home. It seemed so spring like out today. I could hear the birds singing just like in the picture. Wouldn't it have been fun if a bird had landed on my shoulder? We stopped at the bench on Huntington Ave where I first necked with him. He's no Prince Charming but it was a nice way to spend the afternoon.

Friday, March 11, 1938

Chuck came over today and he was smoking a pipe. He looked as though he stepped out of a movie magazine .It's so funny how something as simple as a pipe can make a boy look like a man.

We went over to the YMCA and decided to play ping pong. I crushed him. I'm not one for letting a man win just to boost his ego. If he doesn't have a healthy ego on his own he's not worth having.

After Chuck went home I went on a walk by myself. How beautiful it is out tonight. People are beginning to emerge from their homes after hunkering down for the winter. I'm going to throw the windows of my bedroom open when I get home and welcome spring into our house again.

Saturday, March 19, 1938

Margaret came over during the afternoon and we sat in my room and talked about sex. I don't see what all the fuss is over. It's a totally natural thing. She was a little shocked at my attitude, but she began to understand my reasoning. It's a simple biological function of human beings.

Chuck came over tonight and I wasn't expecting him. We played "strip poker" but only just so far. We owed each other things when it got too, too. I still am nuts over him. I think he is still a little annoyed at me about the ping pong game. He has challenged me to another match. If he thinks I'm not going to give it my all he has another thing coming. I'm out to win at everything I do. I give everything my all. He of all people should know that.

Saturday, April 2. 1938

I went downtown with Elly, a new girl at school. She's just moved here from Maine. I squandered $6.00 on a pair of black patent leather sandals. They are darling! What a beautiful day it was today. Spring certainly is treating us well.

I'm doing very well in school. I don't really seem to have to study very much. Mother says I'm like a sponge. I simply absorb knowledge. I do love to learn new things. I think I'm going to ask for a globe for my birthday. I want to see all of the wonderful places there are to visit. I want to make a plan about traveling and see as many hot spots as I can before I die. Paris is first on my list for certain!

Monday, April 18, 1938

The gang gave me a party at Ruth's house. I had a cold but it was still swell. It was nice of Ruth to invite Elly. Mother and Dad had a dozen red roses sent to the house for me. Opening the door and getting a big white box filled with roses was such a thrill. I wonder how long it will be before I receive roses from a man. Not a boy!

I also got a swell pin from Dada. Oh it is lovely, a large topaz stone with small diamond chips around it. Mother was very pleased. I was told to be very careful with it as it is a family heirloom and it is to be handed down to either my oldest daughter, or if I only have sons I'm to hand it down to my first daughter-in-law.

Mother and Dad gave me a new hat and a lovely new coat that I had my eye on at the Sample Shop.

Wednesday, April 20, 1938

Eighteen years old seems so old to me. I'm not a child anymore. I was thinking of this when I was sitting out on our side porch. When the sun hits it just right it warms the room up as though it were July. While I was lost in thought, sipping my ice tea, Chuck appeared. I made him a glass of ice tea and he sat next to me on our "summer davenport" as Mother calls it.

He told me he had fallen hardest for me than any girl he has known. He got very serious and said he thought he was in love with me. We're so young, I don't know.

I have to have a sit down with the girls and see what they have to say about all of this. I know that Ruth would get married in an instant. She has her life all planned out. Mine is so up in the air.

Saturday, April 23, 1938

Chuck was over this afternoon and evening. He bought me two sodas. We had a long talk in the front hall. We both feel the same way about each other but hope we don't get too serious. We are so young and there is so much out there in our futures. I think we are being very wise by taking it slow and cautiously. Too many young people our age jump into early marriage simply because they want to satisfy their physical needs. How perfectly idiotic that is.

Perfect petting tonight.

Saturday, April 30, 1938

Chuck, Mae Thompson and Stanley Lewis came over this afternoon. Chuck was adorable as always. He kissed me while I was getting his coat from the closet. He is so darling. He's very knowledgeable. He knows something about everything. That will take him far I know.

Sunday, May 1, 1938

Today is Chuck's birthday. His parents gave him some money. We went to the show and then out for something to eat. I wonder how many birthdays will I be celebrating with Chuck? We came back to the house and sat on our porch. I sang happy birthday to him and gave him a big kiss.

Mother was a darling and made him an apple pie. His eyes were so big when she brought it into him. She said she would have made him a cake, but she knew how much he enjoyed her pies. She's so thoughtful that way.

Tuesday, May 3, 1938

I didn't see Chuck all day today. I wrote a swell poem for Elly about her heart Jack Masson. I wrote another one called *A Cynic Looks at Life* in blank verse. Poetry is such a beautiful way to express your innermost thoughts and desires. It is also an important way to inspire people to look at life through different eyes.

A Cynic Looks at Life

What is life –
But a series of fleeting moments
Lost-never to return again
The present—massed uncertainty
Desperate-conforming to conflicting schemes
And you-lost in a maddening whirl.
The future-dreaded-inevitable-
Blows that fate might deal-
Shrinking in oneself-

Seeking a haven subline—
Then you find the past—
Visions-idyllic memories-
Tears perhaps-but oh so sweet
Is that which went before.
But then! Your lethargy awakened!
Monotony for an instant lost
By one enchanting glorious dream
Carrying you breathlessly on-on-
On-Till your soul sinks
Sinks to blissful oblivion.

Thursday, May 5, 1938

Bee and I went downtown after school to Shea's Buffalo and saw Tommy Dorsey and his orchestra. Wow! Was it swell. I couldn't keep my feet still; that swing gets me so! My favorite song, *Star Dust*, just killed me!

I told Bee that *Star Dust* is the song I want to dance to at my wedding when my new husband and I walk out onto the dance floor, although, I don't know if Dad will be willing to pay for a large wedding. Most of my friends will probably do something small and intimate.

The lyrics to the song are so beautiful. I feel that they create a painting in your mind. I love to shut my eyes and imagine the stars and the purple sky.

Star Dust

And now the purple dusk of twilight time
Steals across the meadows of my heart
High up in the sky the little stars climb
Always reminding me that we're apart
You wander down the lane and far away
Leaving me a song that will not die
Love is now the stardust of yesterday
The music of the years gone by

Sometimes I wonder why I spend
The lonely night dreaming of a song
The melody haunts my reverie
And I am once again with you
When our love was new
And each kiss an inspiration
But that was long ago
Now my consolation
Is in the stardust of a song
Beside a garden wall
When stars are bright
You are in my arms
The nightingale tells his fairy tale
A paradise where roses bloom
Though I dream in vain
In my heart it will remain
My stardust melody
The memory of love's refrain

Saturday, May 14, 1938

I Went to Elmer's party tonight with Elly. Between Bob and Dick, I had a plenty rare time. They both tried to neck with me but of course I'm true to my one and only love.

I walked home with Ruth because it was such a nice evening, more like late June than May. Everything smells so fresh and new. I can't wait for our lilac bushes to bloom. The bush beneath my bedroom window is so robust. I just know it's going to have more buds than last year.

Warren Wightman wrote a great short story for the Bennett Beacon called *Water is Thick*. I really enjoyed it. It's all about friendship, and how important it is to have someone in your life that you can talk to. Warren is very talented. I'm sure he'll be a published writer someday.

Monday, May 16, 1938

I found out that Chuck took another girl to the Canisius dance Friday night. I'm not going to say or do anything about it, but if it were to happen again there'll be fireworks. And here I was being so faithful to Chuck when I was at Elmer's party the other night. From now on I'm going to do as I please.

To get my mind of my troubles Helen Smith and I went to the movies and saw Errol Flynn in *Adventures of Robin Hood*. It was simply breathtaking. Really Errol is devastating. I guess he'll always be my favorite.

I wish I could meet Errol Flynn someday. I know he lives in California, but I'll get there some day. I don't think it would be an impossible dream. I heard he prefers young girls rather than older women in their mid to late 20's. I fit that bill.

Saturday, May 21, 1938

Some old friends of mine, Francis, Jane, Jean and I drove down to Allegany. We had piles of fun on the way – singing songs and talking about love sweet love. Four other girls met us up there. I fell in the brook and Jane almost followed suite trying to pull me out. There were eight of us sleeping in one cabin. We didn't get to sleep until 3 a.m. We talked and talked all night long. We shared such intimate details about our lives and what we want in this world.

I asked them all what they thought of marriage and how old you should be before you even consider it. We all have such different dreams and aspirations. Everyone seems to be so clear as to what they want to do with their lives. It's funny, only two want to be mothers and wives. I guess times are changing.

I'm so glad that the weather is so warm. It's unusual for May.

Friday, May 27, 1938

No one is home this evening but me. Chuck came over and he thought my tan was the nuts. We got plenty hot. He told me he could never really love a woman unless he was necking and petting with her. I'm not participating so wholeheartedly because of his views. I have my own mind.

Monday, May 30, 1938 – Memorial Day

I drove on another long ride. Betty from next door asked if she could come along. I was happy to have her. She's a sweet girl. She's not very pretty but very kind. She'll make some guy a wonderful wife someday – she's the type.

Thursday, June 2, 1938

Chuck was over this afternoon. He brought his fishing poles with him. He taught me how to cast in the middle of the street. Everybody thought we were wacky. I fall in love with him more every day. He takes time to share his interests with me. It's not all just about necking.

Ruth came over and we decided to go down-town to pick out my class day dress. What a job! I finally found one and it's gorgeous – blue lace, neck cut low and formfitting. After a tiring day Chuck came back over this evening – a perfect cure for anything.

Everything smells so fresh and beautiful outside. This is the very best time of year. I just can't stop thinking about all of the wonderful things that are going to happen to me. My life is a book with so few pages in it that are filled. I am ready to start filling those pages with exciting and new experiences. I want so much out of life, and I know that I am going to get everything I go after. That's just the kind of girl I am.

Friday, June 10, 1938

Class Day: I looked so beautiful. I had so many compliments. I was running around the house feeling like the bell of the ball. My bedroom was filled with the scent of luscious lilacs. I had practically every window in the house open. It smelled so good outside. Lilacs will always and forever remind me of my youth, these joyful days.

Tommy bought blue cornflowers for my hair. They look divine. He's such a sweet dear old friend. I've known him since kindergarten. The dance was perfect, Chuck looked so handsome. I danced every dance but one. I never tired; how could I? I felt as though I was a part of some grand movie whirling around the dance floor with one handsome young man after another. It gets me to thinking, class day will never be again. This moment in time is one to cherish.

My heart is aching. I'm going to miss Bennett so much. It has been my home.

Saturday, June 11, 1938

The elders, Mother and Dad, went over to the Marvin's this evening. I stayed home. Chuck came over, a little the worse for wear after six cans of beer. He was sober enough to do some heavy arguing and some heavenly love making though. Sometimes the two go hand in hand.

When Mother and Dad came home Chuck and I retired to the side porch. Another night of me laying in his arms and listening to the sweet guitar music that our neighbor plays sometimes at night. He plays so well that Chuck and I don't speak. There is no need for words.

Friday, June 17, 1938

Chuck and I talked about marriage on our side porch. It felt natural and right somehow. But then he said maybe I should go out with other fellows, just for the experience so I will have no regrets – makes sense.

Wednesday, June 22, 1938

Listened to Joe Louis and Max Schmelling fight. Gee it was thrilling! Louis knocked Schmelling out in two minutes. I really love a good fight!

I do wish it had lasted a little longer. We had all been looking forward to a" fight night" for quite a while.

Monday, June 27, 1938

Chuck walked me home from school. Honestly I don't know where we'll end up – Chuck being a Catholic and me a Protestant. We can never marry and boy, he's got everything I love and more. He told me tonight that he takes me semi-seriously – that if he took me too seriously he'd be liable to go the whole way with me. He said he knows we may marry someday. I trust him so implicitly.

Tuesday, June 28, 1938

I got a ring from Dada this morning. She is such a dear grandmother. I'm so lucky to have her here with us. She's not very well-versed in matters of the heart. Grandmother Peters is much better with love advice. She's worldlier. Aunt Jean gave me a handbag, pearls (four strands) from Mother! I know I will wear them on my wedding day. I've made out very well with my graduation.

Mother, Dad, Chuck and I played bridge. The windows were open and you could smell the sweet smell of summer. Our lilac bushes are so big and the blossoms are lasting so long. Mother wants to plant a few more bushes in the front of the house and by the side porch. The bush under my bedroom window is deep French purple, my favorite. I love the white lilacs as well. I always pick a large bouquet and put them in our cut glass vase and place them on our

piano. Our house smells so beautiful and loved.

I walked through the school tonight. It was so quite. A few people were cleaning out their lockers. Some kids were saying goodbye to teachers. I had such a lump in my throat. My dear school, I will miss you so.

Wednesday, June 29, 1938

Graduation night, a milestone in my life. Dada went – I was so pleased. She hasn't been feeling well as of late. Chuck couldn't come. He washes dishes at the Mayflower until 3:00 a.m. The family took me to the Statler Bar for cocktails. How elegant I felt.

I guess I'm all grown up now. I'm no longer a school kid. It's time for me to make my way in the world.

Mother looked beautiful in her cream-colored lace dress, and of course Dad was as handsome as ever. Dada went home in a cab after the ceremony; she was tired out from the excitement, or so I thought. When we got home she had made a lovely spread, thank goodness, I was famished.

Mother and I stayed up quite late and talked about so many things. I'm so glad that I'm an only child. I would hate to share her affection with anyone else. I know how selfish that sounds, but she agreed.

Saturday, July 2, 1938

The proofs of my pictures came today. I don't think they're so hot, but the finished pictures will no doubt be better. Chuck is in Canada, how I miss him. I wrote a smooth poem tonight. He inspires me so.
Thought by Night

When night time comes in silence creeping,
Creeping slowly through the room,
My thoughts to you in bliss are drifting,
Drifting through the peaceful gloom—
Each thing you said, each look you gave,
Deep down within my heart I save—
Each treasure studded with my tears
Which I Shall keep down through the years,
Then just before my eyes are closing,
Closing into dreams of you
My heart is occupied in hoping,
Hoping you're thinking of me too.

Monday, July 4, 1938

My finished pictures came in and they look swell, especially the tinted ones. I'm so glad I put the cornflowers in my hair. It added just the right touch.

We listened to *Lights Out* with Boris Karloff. Mother insists that we always have the lights out when it's on. It makes it all so suspenseful. It was funny though. It was coming to a very scary part of the story. You could tell by the way the music was leading us. All of the sudden some kids had lit a bunch of fire-crackers and the street in front of our house was all lit up with snaps, bangs and pops. I thought Mother and Dada were going to have heart attacks.

I saw Chuck and his family at the drug-store tonight. His mother never seems to smile at me, but his father does.

Saturday, July 16, 1938

Chuck was over this morning and stayed for lunch. I love the way he breezes in, kisses me on the lips and strolls in the kitchen without a care in the world. He feels so comfortable in our home. Mother enjoys it when he gives her a light hug as well. He had to leave to help his father with some chores. I went up in my bedroom and sat at my dressing table and wrote another swell poem.

Swift is the End

O darling, time is flying
We are young and love is new,
Each kiss is just as thrilling
As the first one that we knew.

All the time my heart is sighing,
For I know t'will all be through
When comes the time for parting
From ecstasy and you.

Young love is always burning
With a passion that is real,
But it has the quickest ending
Of emotions that we feel.

So while the flame is ling'ring

Hold me tight—don't let me go.
It's a lifetime that we're living—
We've so few hours you know.

Chuck was able to come back over after dinner. Mother said he might as well have his mail delivered here. Mother and Dad went to the movies tonight giving us the house to ourselves. Dada was over at Mrs. Brown's playing bridge. Chuck and I took advantage of our time alone and made love a lot. I love the way he smells – so clean and masculine.

Monday, July 25, 1938

I feel like a never keeping a diary again. Chuck got hold of it today and tore some of the pages out. He wanted to see how much I like Don. He really is quite jealous. Anyway all is patched up right now.

Oh, I got a post card from Harold up in Isle LeMotte. It sure brought back fond memories. What a sensual summer that was; one for the memory books. Swimming nude is so lovely and relaxing.

Monday, August 1, 1938

I went downtown to luncheon with Mother. I bought three bottles of toilette water. We took a cab and wore our loveliest outfits. Mother lent me a pair of her white gloves from Paris. We shopped for most of the afternoon and then stopped for a much needed cocktail at the Saturn Club. Ruth had promised to meet us there in the courtyard.

What heaven it is walking through the doors of the Saturn Club, such history, such elegance. Dave came over as soon as we sat down and asked us what we would care to drink. He said that Ruth had called ahead of time and asked him to convey her apologies as she was running a bit behind, but that he was to accommodate us until she arrived.

We both ordered side cars. I confided in Mother how my romance with Chuck is a closed book and that I have no regrets. The look on her face was priceless. She had no idea that I was angry with him. He hasn't called in days and is taking me for granted. No man will take me for granted ever.

Ruth came in wearing the most darling yellow cocktail dress. She always knows the perfect thing to wear. I take it that Dave knows exactly what she drinks as all she did was raise her eyebrows and give him a slight smile and he went right to making her a drink. A sidecar as well. Great minds think alike.

When I got home I wrote yet another lovely poem. Poetry allows me to release my feelings and not bottle them up. So many feelings run through my mind. Poetry is a beautiful way to get them all out. I can't keep them inside. I want to share my thoughts with the world. Edna St. Vincent Millay is my favorite poet. I love the way she expresses herself.

Epilogue to Love

Like sunset fading into night
Our love that once was all aglow,
Has swiftly passed right out of sight,
And all the joys we used to know.

A beautiful book must end sometime—
Our story of love is just the same—
A page of tears to make it shine,
And lots of laughter without shame.

A page just filled with mad desire,
And thrills of youth's wild ecstasy—
The book is closed but still the fire
Of love will flame in memory.

Deborah Peters 1938

Monday, August 8, 1938

I have completely forgotten Chuck. It all seems like a dream. Don came over and took me to the Wishing Well for a beer. We sat in a booth and talked about where we wanted our lives to go. Eighteen is such a strange age. We aren't children anymore, but we can live lives as adults; so many rules and restrictions. Who made up those rules anyway? We stopped by the well on our way out and we both threw a penny in. I can't imagine what Don's wish was, but mine was about changing the rules. Afterwards we sat in the car and talked until 2 a.m. He fascinates me beyond words.

Friday, August 12, 1938

Don came over while I was taking a bath. I'm so mad I missed him. I wish Mother would have come up and tapped on the door to tell me. He said he couldn't wait but he left his card. Mother thought it was darling of him.

I found out that Chuck is back on his old job at the gas station. Don told me that Chuck asked him about me. He wants to know what my attitude is towards him. I don't give a damn. I like Don ten times more than I did Chuck.

And Chuck always smell like gasoline, not matter how much he scrubs his hands.

Monday, August 15, 1938

I got my license today and am I thrilled. Don came over to see how I came out. He let me drive his car over to Bee's house. It rode simply swell.

Don told me that Chuck is buying a car. He's paying $25.00 for a Ford Roadster, also Chuck is throwing a drinking party this weekend. It's an end of the summer celebration.

I truly hope Chuck grows up some time soon. He has a long way to go. I know it's the right thing that we have gone our separate way.

Wednesday, August 17, 1938

Don was at my house when I got home. He kissed me twice. His technique is naturally a letdown after Chuck, but that can't be helped. Anybody would be a letdown after Chuck's obvious talent for love making. I'm certain that Don will improve rapidly under my tutelage. After all, he's only seventeen.

Wednesday, August 24, 1938

The weather is unseasonably cold out. Don didn't come over at all today. Mother and I got to talking about him and we both agree that he is a very cold proposition. It takes liquor to warm him up. I wonder if I could change that conceited and cool manner of his. I do like him a lot, but he's not affectionate enough for me.

Mother pointed out that there is a great deal of fish in the sea. I don't have to settle on just one right now. I'm young, I should enjoy myself.

Monday, August 29, 1938

I went to secretarial school today. I bought $25.00 worth of beautiful books for class. I met two swell girls, Alta and Kay. Mother picked me up and we went shopping. I bought a new blue sweater and some darling shoes.

How I wish I were going to college for some wonderful degree. I wish Dad would change his mind.

Friday, September 2, 1938

I understand accounting a lot better. I nearly died with cramps in school. I had to take the bus home today.

Don and some of the kids came over tonight to say goodbye. They were all talking about college. I sure will be blue when they all leave. How different things will be. We were all sitting on the side porch when all of the sudden I thought my heart was going to stop, right then and there. Chuck came around the corner with some beer and a very tentative look on his face.

I played it smooth by asking him why I hadn't seen him in so long, and he said he wasn't sure how he'd be received. I was cordial to him, not overly friendly. He stayed for two beers and then said he had to head home.

After he left I asked Bob how Chuck's affairs of the heart were and Bob said, "I guess he still likes you." Of course I don't know how true any of that is. I'll have to watch and wait.

Saturday, September 10, 1938

Dad mixed up some rare Highballs for all of us and I got in a real silly mood. In fact, Don carried me over to the davenport after we all played bridge. Don and I were out in the kitchen in the dark. He was so swell. He had his arms around me. I told him I would miss him very much when he went back to Duke. Then he kissed me with some real improvement.

I still am in doubt about my positon in his affections. I know I shall cry after he goes. When he's down at Duke he will no doubt forget all about me. I don't wonder with so many attractive girls around. I shall never fight to get him for no man is worth it. He can pursue me but nix on the vise versa.

I still don't understand what happened with my relationship with Chuck. Love at this age is do darn difficult to figure out.

Wednesday, September 14, 1938

I met Bee, Elly and Ginger and a girl from Middlebury who is a friend of Bee's and we saw *Carefree* with Ginger Rogers and Fed Astaire. It was swell. I do wish I could dance as effortlessly as Ginger does. I was thinking of taking dance lessons. Mother said that I have natural rhythm and I don't really need them. I know it would be an expense that we could do without, but it would be such fun. Ruth took them, but then again she can afford to.

Afterwards we had supper at Laube's Old Spain. I splurged 85 cents on chicken ala king. It was divine and well worth it.

My typing is improving. Mother and Dad are very proud. Of course I'm very pleased about that. I know how important it is to them that I succeed in life and become independent. They are truly wonderful parents.

Honestly I'm going nuts thinking about Don all the time and wondering about the future. How strange the future is. It's out there in front of all of us just waiting to come to life. Yet there is so much talk of war. There is always that uneasy feeling within me – that sweet pain about everything. Oh well that's life at 18.

Saturday, September 17, 1938

Mother and I went to see Norma Shearer and Tyrone Power in *Marie Antoinette*. I never cried so hard in all my life. It was two hours and four minutes long and simply gorgeous. And oh! How beautiful Norma Shearer was! The love scenes were terrific and the acting superb. I've talked of nothing else all day – ah to love like that and never to marry – how cruel. I spoke to Ruth tonight and we discussed *Marie Antoinette*. She agreed that
love like that is dead; more's the pity.

I had cocktails with Mother and Dad when I got home. We had a simple salad and some chicken for dinner. I was so hungry.

Monday, September 15, 1938

Bee was over this afternoon and we got to talking about Chuck and the whole darn mix-up when, speaking of the devil, Chuck and Mitch drove up in Chuck's old Ford. We went for a ride and I sat up front with Chuck and Mitch and Bee sat in the rumble seat. It sure was a wild ride and my hair was blown to pieces.

After they dropped us off, Bee headed home. It is such a perfect day. I love the fall with all of its rich colors.

This evening the doorbell rang and there was Chuck again. I asked him in and he stayed for an hour. He is still the same rare person. I don't know what his game is, but whatever it is he won't get far. He's hard to resist but I have to keep my resolve.

Tuesday, September 20, 1938

My typing continues to improve. I seem to have a flair for it. Today in law class an auto went by with the radio playing *Day Dreaming*. I really went nuts hearing it. Those lyrics were so perfect for that moment.

DAYDREAMING (ALL NIGHT LONG)
(Words by: Johnny Mercer / Music by: Harry Warren)
Sung by: Rudy Vallee and Rosemary Lane

All night long I'm day-dreaming
Day-dreaming of wonderful you
Constantly I can see you before me
Then we kiss and you whisper you adore me
And though I know I'm only day-dreaming
Please tell me I'm not play-dreaming
Tell me I'm not wrong
While I'm day-dreaming all night long.

Tonight the news flashes are all about the Czech Crisis. Germany has stated a deadline (Thursday 3 p.m.) for Czech's decision to surrender or defend itself. Britain and France want Czechoslovakia to surrender but I don't think they should. I hope Russia defends Czechoslovakia and wipes Germany out and also Hitler's mustache.

Bee was down tonight and we had one of our many confidential talks, one of the nicest parts of a girl's life.

Wednesday, September 21, 1938

Czechoslovakia surrendered this morning. I think it was all very foolish; Hitler is just bluffing and if England, France and Russia had declared to defend the Czechs, Hitler would have been scared stiff. I hope all those so-called powers realize that after Hitler has Czechoslovakia he will have that many more men to fight for him. Not that Czechs ever would fight for Hitler.

Saturday, September 24, 1938

Mother has made a leopard-cloth jacket. I wore it with my black dress and it looks stunning. She bought some beautiful material to make a dress for me to wear at Christmas. It has a black background with bits of red and a touch a green. Mother can make her own patterns. She should have been a dress designer. I'm missing Don more and more. If he comes home at Christmas and doesn't know I'm alive I shall simply die.

The war scare in Europe is tense. Each country is mobilizing its troops and Czechoslovakia is going to resist Germany, which I think is very courageous. The British are demanding a firm stand in the crisis to be taken by this government.

What is going to happen to this world? This is such a frightening time. I pray every night for peace to come into the minds of these men who have the ability to discuss instead of fight.

Tuesday, September 27, 1938

School is still swell but when I get home I still miss Don. There was an item in the travelogue of the society page about Don and two other fellows returning to Duke. I am listening to the radio right this very minute. I'm at my dressing table and the window is slightly ajar. You can hear all of the other neighbors listening too. We are waiting for important news flashes from Europe. Everybody is on edge waiting for the bomb to explode. We should all pray very hard tonight.

Thursday, September 29, 1938

The war has been averted. Hitler, Mussolini, Daladier and Chamberlin have signed an agreement. Thank God!

I had a dream about Don last night and boy was it smooth. I can't wait to see him again. I'm listening to *Why'd You Make Me Fall In Love With You?* It's as though it was written just for Don and me. Music can take you places and lift your mood so easily. When I'm down I will lie on my bed and close my eyes and imagine Don standing right next to me. Music makes it all so real.

Friday, September 30, 1938

This sure was my lucky day. When I got home I found a letter from Don. Gee! It was swell! He signed it "Avec Amour" which is pretty nice for him.

Chuck came over this evening and we played some bridge. He took me to Mann's in that car of his. I had five scotch and sodas and Chuck had five rye highballs. We went for a ride afterwards. He's really a swell person come to think of it.

Mother was up when I got home and she made me a small plate to eat. She took one look at me and realized I needed to put something in my stomach.

Saturday, October 1, 1938

Chuck was over late this evening. At first he was impossible, but then he said something that made me cry and we got real serious. I told him that I never said a thing against him after our affair ended. He said that he broke off with me because he thought we were getting in a little too deep and I had said that we could never get married.

He really was so swell that he just about broke my heart. He also said that it took everything for him to stay away. Well it may have all been a line to make me feel better but it was perfect anyway. So I'll take it at face value. He said he would still be coming over but not too frequently for our own good.

Friday, October 7, 1938

I typed two perfect letters at school today. I was thrilled. During lunch hour I bought a new hat, a beautiful black felt and alpine style with two brown pheasant feathers and a blue ostrich feather too. It's darling and will go swell with my blue suit.

The papers are full of football. The odds are 7-5 that Duke will beat Colgate. I hope so. Some of the Duke team was in the paper tonight. They are swell-looking guys. I have all my homework done for the weekend so I can thoroughly enjoy myself.

Dad is all geared up for the game.

Saturday, October 8, 1938

I never was so thrilled in my life as I was at the game. Both Duke's and Colgate's bands were wonderful. The game was marvelous. Duke won 7-0. However, they didn't score until the third quarter; a real nail biter. I was pretty worried because Colgate put up such a swell battle. Anyway I yelled my head off for the Blue Devils, and they came through. I bought a big Duke Banner.

Sunday, October 9, 1938

Dada had a coronary stroke early this morning. She is very seriously ill and can't be moved from the davenport. She can't speak because the effort is too great and when she tries to write the words are all jumbled. Aunt Milly is coming over all day administering hypos, and Mother is a nervous wreck. What a day!

Margaret said she found out from Leroy that Don once said I was so much fun and was always the same, day after day. He said I was never in a bad mood. I'm retiring to the Duke banner on my wall.

Wednesday, October 12, 1938

As I look in last year's entry I think of the long way Chuck and I have come from that night when everything was a lark. He came over and we celebrated our anniversary. It is the most gorgeous autumn night I've ever seen. It is as warm as summer and the moon and stars are shinning so bright and clear just for us. We walked through Central Park through the leaves and then sat down by a fountain. It seemed as if tonight was forever. We couldn't help ourselves. His arms were the same and always will be, so were his kisses. Tonight was worth it. We can hold it in our memory for the rest of our lives. Oh why, oh why does it have to end?

Thursday, October 13, 1938

All day I've thought about last night. I really know Chuck now for the really swell person that he is. We tried so hard last night but that old feeling came back. We'll never forget each other I know. He told me that girl over the summer was a rebound romance to help him forget me. He hasn't seen her in two months. I think he is still nuts about me. But it's just one of those things – the wall is there, and we can't surmount it.

Friday, October 15, 1938

The weather continues to be simply perfect. I thought about Don and Chuck all day today. I like them in different ways: Chuck for the down to earth romance that thrills and delights me. Don for the aesthetic kind of dreamy and idealistic way that he looks at life. I'm so glad I surrendered the other night with Chuck. That's really the only way to get anything out of life. The pain of first love will always remain I know. It's a beautiful thing and nothing you do seems wrong. Oh! Eighteen is a perfect age.

Sunday, October 23, 1938

Duke had their fifth straight win last Friday. I'm so bored I think I'm going to go crazy. I look so nice today, and of course there is not a male around.

I wrote another smooth poem about that night Chuck and I took that long walk. Gee! I wish he'd come over tonight and take me for another one. I would sit with him and recite my poem to him:

October Night

The autumn leaves-they tumble down
The sultry air-it filled the night,
A wistful moon-it made a crown
Of beauty everywhere in sight.

We walked among the rustling leaves—
They whispered of our slumbering love,
The moon and stars-they seemed to call
To us and say: Take back your long-lost love.

When old October comes again
To clothe the world in loveliness,
Then we'll be walking down the lane
In one brief hour of breathlessness.

The memory of that perfumed night
Is ours to share forevermore,
And it will burn with poignant light
Although our paths may cross no more.

Here I am looking forward to Christmas vacation when Don comes home – I hope he comes over often while he's home.

I seem to be fighting with myself between two loves. I need to give one of these romances my all. Dividing love can never work. I have to give this a great deal of thought and consideration and make my mind up once and for all.

Wednesday, October 26, 1938

Dada had her best day. She is very bright and has said a lot of new words. Mother and I are going to a fashion show and bridge party at the Church of the Good Shephard. We always enjoy seeing the new fashions, and Mother gets great ideas for new clothes to make for me.

Halloween, Monday, October 31, 1938

Mother is nuts about her new hat, and I love mine too. They certainly are stunning. Chuck was there when we arrived home. He has to wear glasses for reading. He sure looks rare in them. He is still smoking that pipe of his. Now with the glasses on he looks like a professor. He is so handsome I can't contain myself.

When he was leaving I held his coat for him and he said, "I wish I could do over again everything I've done in this coat." I know what he meant, and it surely was sweet to hear him say it.

I do miss being little at Halloween. It was always such fun to get all dressed up and be whoever you wanted to be.

The street is filled with the sounds of children running from house to house collecting their treats. Mother made her famous chocolate chip cookies and wrapped them up in little fabric bags she made out of orange and black cloth that was left over in her sewing basket.

Chuck came back at 11:00, and we had scotch and sodas around the corner and then a darling kitten followed us home so I put him in our cellar for the night. Gee I wish we could keep it but Dad has allergies. I'll see if Laura would like to adopt her.

Tuesday, November 1, 1938

Dad doesn't know we have the kitten in the basement. Mother adores it. We call her "Weiner," because we found her on Halloween. We won't be able to keep her forever. I don't want to part with her. She's so very small and helpless. She has orange fur with a small white spot on the middle of her forehead and her paws are all white too.

Dada sat up for quite a while today. The doctor was over and is satisfied with her condition.

I went early Christmas shopping today. I bought some Francis Denny Cologne for Dada and a slip for Mother. I know what kind of perfume I want for Christmas, Apropos, it's simply luscious by Anjou. I'll have to walk Mother by the fragrance counter next time we are downtown.

Friday, November 18, 1938

Rained like all hell in the beginning of the day. I had the car and the windshield wipers could barely keep up with the rain. Dad let me have the car as long as I drove him into work. He's getting a ride home from a co-worker.

Laura and I went downtown and saw Tyrone Power in *Suez,* and it sure was super. I'm getting to like Tyrone more and more – what a determined jaw, and those dreamy eyes!

On our way home the traffic was slow, and it started to snow, big heavy flakes. Pretty, but not fun to drive in.

Sunday, November 20, 1938

When I woke up this morning I thought of Chuck. He certainly gives the most thrilling kisses in the cleanest way, so superior to those awful soul kisses. I think I could go the world over and no man could make love like he does.

I wrote to Don this afternoon. I'm still uncertain about my love life. I listened to "Romeo & Juliet" the music was glorious. Tchaikovsky's Romeo & Juliet stirs romantic longings all right and some real urges too.

Thursday, November 24, 1938 – Thanksgiving

Terribly cold and very white Thanksgiving. Chuck and Don came over this afternoon. Chuck told us that he has a date with Marla Bailey tonight, and of all the cheap little sluts. Really he should do better than that. Who goes out with a fellow on Thanksgiving anyway?

Swell dinner at the Marvins. I actually felt ill I ate so much. Dad mixed some swell cocktails. We were all so happy that Dada was able to come. We stayed until 10:15 – this was good for her being out of the house.

I do love Thanksgiving so much. It's all simply about being grateful for what you have. I love this time of year, heading into Christmas. I have to make my list of what I would like to have under the tree. Of course I love surprises too.

I think I would like to make some gifts this year, but they would have to be very nice ones.

Saturday, December 3, 1938

Mother had an upset stomach. I did the breakfast and lunch dishes. I read *The Citadel* aloud to Dada tonight. She enjoyed it so. I truly feel she is getting better. Even the doctor agrees with me.

Saturday, December 10, 1938

Mother and Dad went out with the Reeses to a show and the Athletic Club. Not bad!
The unexpected happened tonight. Chuck came over looking super. I made a resolution at the beginning of the evening that I would not give in. Well after two hours of struggling I finally did. I just couldn't help it. And all of the time Don was in the back of my mind. His name seemed seared into my brain. What would he think if he knew etc. Still I guess it's to be expected. You can't cheat yourself all of the time. I thought Chuck would never "get" me again, but tonight he was the Chuck of old – tender – loving – perfect and like a small boy.

Tuesday, December 13, 1938

All of my gifts are piled up in the back of my closet ready to place under the tree. I do so hope everyone likes what I got them. I like to take time and pick out just the right gift. I found the perfect gift for each person in record time.

I've made myself a cup of tea to help keep me warm as I sit hear writing. Mother is humming a Christmas tune downstairs. I can't quite make out what it is, but I'm certain that it's a Christmas song. I had a sudden chill; Dada says when that happens someone is walking over your grave.

There was, and still is, a terrible blizzard. The wind is going 66 miles an hour. I can hear it rattling my bedroom window as I am writing this. It reminds me of *Wuthering Heights*, when Cathy is out on the moors in the blizzard calling for Heathcliff. I do wish I could shake this chill.

Wednesday, December 21, 1938

I got up around 10:30 a.m. and was looking out the bathroom window when suddenly a cherry red coupe drove up and Don jumped out. Well, I never dressed so fast before in my life, and I flew down the stairs. He looked perfectly darling, only very tired. He and his roommate left Durham yesterday and drove all last night and got in town about 8:00 a.m.

Well I think I'm doing pretty good – he came over to see me pretty quickly. We fought as usual and Mother was so nervous she burned a batch of cookies. He hasn't changed a bit since summer and I'm really glad. His sister is going to have a baby in the spring so Don will be and uncle. So funny to think of him in a role like that.

Saturday, December 24, 1938

Don was over this afternoon. Perfect. Said he'd almost bought me two decks of cards in Durham with pictures of Duke on them.

Our tree is beautiful – a scotch pine and absolutely spell binding. Our liquor consists of Haig & Haig scotch - twelve years old, bottled side car cocktails, and sherry wine. Wow!

Went to church. Each year it is more beautiful and inspirational. It fills my heart with love for each person there. We pray together and you can feel God listening to each one of us.

When I got back Mother and Dad went over to a party at the Marvins. Dada went to bed early. She's feeling very tired lately. I pray that she will be with us next year at this time.

Don came just as they were leaving, and we sat in the glorious light of the tree and talked. He gave several Christmas kisses. He was wonderful. Then we went to Mann's and had a scotch and a roast beef sandwich. Got in at quarter to two.

Sunday, December 25, 1938 Christmas Day

Each year seems more perfect. I got so much. Toilette water, perfume, underwear, beautiful sea green satin housecoat, stunning evening slippers, Van Roalte stockings, angora mittens (red), matching angora jacket, rhinestone bracelet, pink satin nightgown, silk blouse, Coty set, and to top it all a golf bag and set of six clubs, from Dad. I nearly died I was so surprised.

The cocktails and wine were swell, and the dinner was grand. Only I ate so much turkey I couldn't eat any plum pudding. The table setting was lovely as always. The china is so delicate you can almost see through the plates. And the crystal, I feel like a queen sitting here sipping out of these glasses. My favorite is the silver candlesticks in the center of the table and the centerpiece of pine and holly. Aunt Kate called up long distance. P.S. Don wasn't over all day.

Tuesday, December 27, 1938

I didn't see Don but I don't wonder there is so much snow outside. I don't want Dad to shovel. Mr. Slatter, our butcher, had a heart attack last week and died. He was two years younger than Dad.

I wrote to Aunt Kate this afternoon. Weiner was over today with Laura. He climbed half way up the Christmas tree and Dad was so mad. Bee ventured out into the storm to come down and see me. What a wonderful friend.

Mother has fixed my blue lace for tomorrow night. It's sort of off the shoulder and extremely low in the neck. I've put four rhinestone clips on it. It sure looks the nuts and with my new evening slippers. Wow!

Wednesday, December 28, 1938

Mitch, Don and Chuck were over for bridge. It was swell until Chuck started acting up. I was so nervous my hands shook. Chuck and Mitch seem to be trying to queer me with Don and vice versa. They're dangerous. We had a riot with the mistletoe. Don gave me a short kiss and dashed out. My gardenias came from Elmer while the kids were here. I hope Don was jealous.

The dance was swell. It was so very formal. All of the girls looked so beautiful and the music was magical. Elmer is a divine dancer. My perfume got to all the boys. I met Tommy's girlfriend Isabel Barker. It's a good thing she's got money. We had cocktails at the Touraine after. I got home at 3:45 a.m.

Saturday, December 31, 1938

Laura came over for a while to wish us a Happy New Year. She had Weiner with her. I made a little pre-party for her and lit the fire and we sat in front of the tree. I gave her a very small glass of wine to toast the New Year. She helped me bring out the spread Mother had prepared: shrimp and cocktail sauce, cheeses and crackers and her famous cake cookies with chocolate frosting.

My guests arrived and Laura stayed for a while. I'm glad she did, she seemed a little lonely. It's a good thing she didn't stay for long. I think she felt bad because she dropped a shrimp on the carpet with cocktail sauce on it. Mother would have had a fit if she knew. Laura didn't know that I saw it happen. It doesn't really matter, everything blends into an oriental carpet. As I said, I'm glad she didn't stay; things got pretty out of hand.

Here's the story: Don, Lloyd and Mitch came over with Ginger around 10:00 p.m. We started the night off with some of the peach brandy that Lloyd's father made. Then we had scotch and sodas, and the drinking continued from there. Don started necking with Ginger. I never saw anything like him. He sure was under the influence or he would never have acted the way he did.

All of the sudden he spanked me and practically ripped my blouse. Mitch told him to stop. I was so nervous that Mother and Dad would come downstairs and see what was going on. Dad would have had a fit and thrown Don out on his ear. Thankfully we all came out of it and got around to playing bridge from 3:00 a.m. until 5:00 a.m. Wow!

Sunday, January 1, 1939

I slept fine but my stomach felt shaky all day. Don went home with Dad's coat on last night. Dad said Don appeared to be pretty the worse for wear. He was over this afternoon to return Dad's coat, and he looked terrible and didn't remember anything of what happened last night.

Ginger called up and said that she has Don's ring – what he said no girl would ever get. I hope he gets it back.

I don't think I will ever be able to look another scotch and soda in the face again. I'd have to say the rarest thing about last night was opening the champagne and it shooting all over the kitchen walls.

Thursday, January 5, 1939

Chuck was over tonight. I guess he still likes me. I let go tonight. I might as well. I guess being a nice girl doesn't pay if New Year's Eve is a sample. However, the fact still remains I still love Don as he was last summer – ideals and what goes with them! I finished my homework after Chuck left. I laid in my bed and read *Camille* for a while. It's so romantic.

I also looked over my diary for all of the entries made during the summer. I saw Don 50 times!! It doesn't seem possible. He must have liked me. The summer all seems like a dream that is slipping out of my fingers. Those nights were so perfect and such a different Don from the Don of New Year's Eve.

I wonder if I'll see the Don of last summer again.

Sunday, January 8, 1939

I went to communion with Laura. She is such a dear and very pretty too. She'll have the boys buzzing around her door just like her older cousin.

It was very restful being in church. This afternoon Laura and I went to the movies to see Joan Crawford in *The Shining Hour*. Perfectly swell. It's amazing how much the movies can take you away from yourself – how they give you something to think about.

Over these last few days how much Chuck has been on my mind. His good points have been magnified. He's so tender and sweet and yet dynamic. As for loving, he'd make a perfect husband. I know!

Thursday January 12, 1939

I went to the movies with Carol. It was the second time I saw *The Sisters* but oh! Errol Flynn is worth seeing again and again. I nearly died he's so wonderful. There ought to be a law against men like that. It makes me very dissatisfied with my routine existence. I was born for just such exciting romance. Who knows? Maybe someday I'll meet a man like he portrayed and have just such a whirlwind courtship.

Saturday, January 14, 1939

Gee! It was swell sleeping in this morning! I dusted my room, took a bath and washed my underwear, also shoveled the front walk. I have no idea where all of this energy is coming from.

I'm wearing my hair in a new way, short curls brushed off my forehead flat on top of my head. This eliminates the center part; which is not good for a slender face.

I read *The Three Musketeers* all evening. It is super smooth; very exciting and romantic. I can't make up my mind which one of the Musketeers I would be most interested in. They are all very intriguing.

I tried on the nightgown I got for Christmas. It looks perfect and fits my figure to a "T." I look like a bride on her wedding night.

Monday, January 16, 1939

Chuck called up then came over. He looked smooth when he walked through the door. He seemed more confident than ever. We played bridge, and Dad gave us some 12-year-old scotch. Wow!

I still like Chuck a lot and after all why not make the best of my opportunities now that Don is somewhat in the background. I sure did tonight!

Tuesday, January 17, 1939

I saw *The Citadel*. It was perfectly marvelous. I love reading the book first and seeing the movie later on. The movie lived up to the book. Robert Donat is so handsome and soft spoken. And I adore Rosalind Russell. She is such a strong woman and great actress. This movie will always remind me of how I would read *The Citadel* to Dada at night. It was such a special time for both of us.

When I got home Dad said Ginger had phoned me so I called her up fully expecting her
to say she'd had a letter from Don. Well, nary a word about him. She asked me out to the Wanakah Country Club on Saturday. I accepted. Why not? You might as well get the most out of people. I can't keep on being perfect.

Saturday, January 21, 1939

I had a swell time at the Wanakah Club with Ginger and Jan and Bonnie, two of her friends. We played badminton and sang songs and also indulged in the fine art of drinking. I had two scotch and sodas which were bar excellence.

Before going out Ginger and I bought some foreign cigarettes, Salem which are perfumed and Hellman's which are Egyptian. They were very strong. Though I don't like Ginger, she fascinates me. She didn't say she had heard from Don at all, only she talked a little about New Year's Eve.

Wednesday, January 25, 1939

The secretarial school had a Mother & Daughter tea at the YWCA residence. It was the nicest tea I ever attended. The residence is a beautiful place. I introduced Mother to a lot of the girls. I'm so proud of her. We were sorry to leave, but I had plans at 4:00.

Chuck came over and brought two small bottles of cognac and scotch. That cognac is plenty potent stuff. He didn't get here until 5:00. An hour late doesn't do him any favors. I was terribly tired and wanted to go to bed but Chuck made me so mad – he wouldn't go and believe me I said a few things to make him mad.

I don't like it when I lose my temper. I always try my best to remain in control. Chuck just makes it so difficult some times.

Friday, January 27, 1939

Our shorthand test was terrible. I didn't get a good mark at all, I know.

Life is so damn dull, I'm going crazy. Chuck called up and said he might be over. I said suppose someone else calls me up? Well that made him mad I guess, because he said goodbye and hung up very quickly. I guess I ruin everything for myself.

All I want is excitement. There are so many things to see and hear. I am in this awful place getting nowhere fast.

Tuesday, January 31, 1939

It was snowing again this morning; big white flakes that floated down out of the sky that you could catch with the tip of your tongue. Pretty, but it took me an hour to get to school. The buses were all jammed to capacity. I never saw so much snow in all my life. When I got home from school Chuck's car was stuck in the snow out in front of our house. I steered as he dug it out of the rut.

The Browns were here for supper. On cold blizzard nights it's grand having the neighbors over. Mrs. Brown brought over warm rolls out of the oven and cookies as their contribution.

After dinner we sat in the living room and Dad made a big fire and we shared our hopes for the New Year.

Bee came over and we went up in my room. We sat on the floor and lit a candle. We spent the evening talking about sex – not a very unusual conversation for this age of 18. I hate being in the dark about so many things, but who to ask? Mother is a dear, but there are areas I dare not tread with her.

Thursday, February 2, 1939

Bee and I saw the first star of 1939, John Garfield in, *They Made Me A Criminal*. He was truly wonderful, and I could see it again and again. John Garfield has this very earthy quality that simply draws you in to a picture. He's not pretty like Errol Flynn; he's magnetic.

I got home to find that Chuck had been here. I guess he must really like me even if necking and stuff are out. I can't kiss him one day and be aloof to him the next. It isn't fair to him.

Valentine's Day is coming up and it's one of my least favorite holidays. Someday I'm going to get a dozen long stem red roses delivered to my door from the man of my dreams.

Sunday, February 12, 1939

I made a swell cake today, chocolate with double chocolate frosting. I love how domestic I feel working alone in the kitchen. I put the radio on and danced about with Mother's apron on. Simple pleasures I guess.

Aunt Helen, Mother, Carol, Laura and I went to see *Four Daughters*, the picture that John Garfield made famous. It was superb and I cried just as much as I did in *The Sisters*.

We went over to Carol and Laura's tonight, and I had a rare time looking over old snap-shots. I never laughed so hard in my life. We certainly were awful looking prunes in those days. Aunt Helen laughed so much the tears were running down her face. I'm so glad Mother is so close with her sister. Aunt Helen is a peach.

I went up in Carol's room with her, and we sat on her bed and talked. We concentrated on some pretty serious subjects. It was a regular bull session: child birth, death and sex were our main focus.

Tuesday, February 14, 1939

I'm so tired today. Valentine's Day always get me down. When will I have a valentine of my very own? This waiting and wondering is dreadful.

Bee was down tonight. She heard a lecture from a man who talked on youth. He said that petting is inevitable and is perfectly all right because it serves as an emotional background for marriage. Well, that puts a new slant on things. Maybe I should take advantage of his point of view. That's the trouble; there are so many pros and cons on the subject.

Well I think that man is right, but promiscuous petting is out, for me at least.

Wednesday, February 15, 1939

I bought some new pearls for 59 cents, some bargain! They drop just the right length for me too.

I wrote a six-page letter to my friend Jean in New York. Queer how we haven't seen each other in six years and yet we say such intimate things in our letters. I adore having a pen pal.

The family has unanimously decided that Weiner is going to have kittens in about three weeks I guess. I'm terribly excited, and Carol and Laura are thrilled as well. I wish I could keep one of them for my very own. I wish and I wish, but Dad's allergies never go away.

Sunday, February, 19, 1939

My hair looks perfect today. I ran into John Barnes at our youth meeting tonight. He fascinates me. He looks like Cary Cooper, so tall and shy and handsome. Bee says he's fast, but that's what attracts me more. Boy! I'd like to go out with him just to see how far he'd go. Old devil me again!

Very cold out today. I can't think of any reason to like this month. It's always cold and grey.

Friday, February 24, 1939

Lois, Ginger and I went to the show. Chuck called up before I left, and I took great pleasure in saying I had a date.

I found out plenty from Ginger. She had received a post-card and two letters from Don. On the postcard he said he was lit to the gills on scotch and beer all last weekend. Honestly, I don't like him at all now. The only thing I like is the memory of him last summer.

When he gets back, if I see him I'll be nice, but very distant. I have it all planned! Anyway I'm relieved now that I don't care for him. It takes a load off my mind.

Friday, March 3, 1939

School was such a grind today. I want spring fever to hit me soon. Of course winter keeps getting in the way.

Chuck came over tonight. He's just dying to know who has been dating me, but I didn't tell him. I'm sure he'll find out, but he won't get it from me. I'm surprised no one has told him I've been seeing John Barnes.

We played bridge after dinner. Dad and Chuck won. I had a gin concoction before going to bed and boy did I feel it!

I told Chuck that I wanted to find out more about the evils of petting, if there are any, before I continue. He is so darling and pretty hard to resist.

As for John, I wouldn't really say we are dating. I'm only 18. I don't want to be tied down.

Sunday, March 12, 1939

I went over to see Bee this afternoon. While I was gone Chuck came over again. Gee! He sat and talked to Dad about his future and what options he had. When I got home he was so pleased to see me walk through the door. He was darling and in a perfect mood too. I was sorry that I had to go to my youth group, but I simply couldn't miss it.

I had a swell time. John Barnes was there, and I played the piano for him. He has such bedroom eyes. He asked me if I wanted to go see Artie Shaw. I'm thrilled! Artie Shaw is the most handsome band leader there is. He could be a movie star if he wanted to. I'd love to see him on the screen.

I had the car so we went to Mann's for cocktails. I ordered a sidecar and he had a scotch and soda. Things certainly are picking up! However, the boys at youth group aren't very high class and certainly not what I'm used to. There's no harm in accepting one date I feel.

Tuesday, March 14, 1939

I bought another "Modern Library" edition of the Complete Poems of Shelly and Keats. It is a beautiful volume only $1.25

I received a beautiful letter from Tommy. What a sweet, dear old friend he's just like a girlfriend. I think my correspondence with him will live all during my life as one of the most beautiful things in my existence. He gave me a lot of advice with regards to petting. He definitely is against it. It doesn't seem possible that a boy of 19 years of age can be so idealistic.
Added item: Last night Chuck tried to climb up the porch to my bedroom. Queer what boys can do. I'm sure glad he didn't make it! Wink!

Friday, March 17, 1939

I thought a lot about John today. It could develop into something if I let it.

Weiner had her kittens in Carol and Laura's cellar in their laundry bag amidst the noise of plumbers and their rattling pipes.

Mother says they are the most beautiful kittens she has ever seen. I can't wait to have a pet someday. In color they range from dark brown to one just the color of Weiner. She is terribly proud of them.

As much as I love kittens I would love to have a puppy someday. I'd want it to be a big fluffy dog that I could cuddle with and take on long walks. Dogs have such soulful eyes.

Tuesday, March 21, 1939

I went to see Artie Shaw with John. Artie was simply supper. He's as handsome as they come. There were about 4,000 people there, and were they having a good time. John was actually smiling and twirling me around. It did my heart good to see him enjoying himself. He always seems so grim. I'm going to try to get him to dance a little more with me. When he comes over to the house I'm going to put some records on and get him moving.

Thursday, March 23, 1939

I went to Wanakah Country Club with Ginger, Betty and Pete. We had an elegant time playing cards and drinking scotch. I was feeling wonderful after three. Ginger hasn't heard from Don since he sent the postcard. Thank goodness. I shouldn't care, but I do.

All the time we were drinking I was thinking of Don. Naturally his name is synonymous with scotch. Somehow I think I'll be seeing him when he gets home for vacation – sort of a queer premonition.

Thursday, March 30, 1939

Ruth and I went down to the train to meet Florence Miller. I haven't seen her in ages. She certainly is a perfectly swell girl – very natural and unaffected.

I called Ginger tonight. I asked her if she'd seen Don. Lo and behold, he'd been over Sunday, then he took her out Tuesday night (boy am I glad I had a date with John.) Then she told me she is taking him to a dance tomorrow night. I was simply amazed!

She had the nerve to rave about his sophisticated technique and how on Saturday he knew all the dark places to park. Well, I told her I was so proud of the fact that Don had always acted like a perfect gentleman with me. She hesitated for a moment after I said that.

Wednesday, April 5, 1939

Plenty happened during the night. Some drunks went by and threw a stone breaking our sunporch window, and they also busted a big window in the Shelby house across the street.

Mother saw the red car speed down Starin Ave. The police got on the job and when Mitch and Chuck were here this afternoon some detectives came and questioned them. Mitch denied the charges but I think he's guilty because the stone thrown in our window and a stone found in his car are exactly alike. The detectives hauled both of them off to police headquarters for further questioning.

Dad just wants to make sure someone pays for that broken window on our porch. Mother wants the boys to clean up the mess. Chuck said he would when he's done at the police station.

Thursday, April 6, 1939

I fully expected something to happen today. Mother will not testify against Mitch and Chuck so they got away with it in spite of circumstantial evidence against them. Chuck did come back and clean up the mess with his tail between his legs.

Tommy was in town for a couple of days. He's leaving for Washington tomorrow. How lucky he is to be living in such a vibrant place.

He came over tonight and we stayed up until midnight talking about sex. He sure knows the score. He is going to bring some book over tomorrow on birth control. After reading it I will probably lose all of my romantic ideas.

It's too bad Mitch got out of this business. Mother is too kind-hearted. I wish I was the one who saw that car.

Saturday, April 8, 1939

Mother saw Chuck over at the grocery store. He said no more cops had been to his home. At least our family is still on speaking terms with him. I'm glad because I like him still.

Tommy brought over that book before he left for Washington. It's called Practical *Methods of Birth Control.* It certainly gives all of the glaring details. I guess I'll know the score by the time I finish it.

I wrote a swell poem tonight – Youth vs. War.

How terrible it would be if our country went to war. Mother says that war takes such a toll on young people. It makes them old before their time.

Youth vs. War

Youth looks at life with shining eyes,
Their heritage on one denies
A future bright with each new day,
Their hopes and dreams you can't betray!
When the flaming dawn enfolds the morning sky,
God, let them live! Don't let them die!
Let no shadow cloud that burning dawn,
Let no guns mock the birds' sweet song
Lest on some windswept, foreign field
Their bodies lie all battle-scarred in blood,
No more to love, to laugh, to feel
The goodness of the quiet rain, the flood
Of sunset glow, the deepness of the night;
No cause can justify their flight,
The wine that throbs throughout their veins
Must never soak the rugged plains,
Beauty is youth, and youth is beauty
To die must never be their duty.
Deborah Peters - 1939

Sunday, April 9, 1939 Easter Sunday

Carol, Laura and I all dressed in blue – like spring bluebells. Church service was beautiful this morning. The sun was shining through the stained glass windows, such beautiful vivid colors. Everyone looked so elegant. I love seeing all of the varied Easter bonnets.

Chuck was over this afternoon looking as darling as ever. He really seemed to want to be alone with me.

We had a beautiful dinner with the family over. Carol and Laura brought some Parkside Easter chocolate in a darling basket. How sweet of them to think of us.

Mother made a ham with asparagus, au gratin potatoes, and banana cake with cream cheese frosting. Oh how I love the holidays! The house was filled with the fragrance of hyacinths. We had pink, blue and deep purple ones. Our crisp white linen table cloth with napkins to match set off our family china and crystal so perfectly.

Tuesday, April 11, 1939

Bee was over tonight. We had a long intimate talk together. She thinks I have done plenty well with John. I pray that it continues. He was at youth group last night, and he sat next to me. He looked low, and I asked him if anything was wrong. He told me that his father is out of a job so that's why he is working so hard and such long hours. No wonder he hasn't asked me for another date. Afterward he walked all the way with me. This is the strangest boy I ever knew; such a cynic. When we got to my house I drove him home. Was I surprised when he kissed me good night! At last!

The kittens are so darling. Laura brought them over for Mother to cuddle with. I just want to squeeze them. They are walking quite well now on their own. They keep looking at you with their big blue eyes.

I have several letters that I must catch up on. I am so far behind in my correspondence.

Thursday, April 13, 1939

I cleaned out my bureau drawers. I love it when my room is all in order.

I got another postcard from Tommy. He said that Washington is so beautiful this time of year. It's much warmer there than it is here of course. The cherry blossoms will be out very soon. Oh how I would love to live there. Lilacs and Cherry Blossoms are my favorite.

I've been thinking a great deal about John. He seems so dour and sad all the time. I wonder what he is keeping hidden inside that makes him that way. His father is still out of a job. I'm sure that weighs heavily on him. He is the breadwinner of the house, and he's only 19. He's so tall and handsome.

Saturday, April 15, 1939

I cleaned my room and closet, made my bed, washed and dried some underwear and now I'm exhausted.

I listened to the radio in the living room and dreamed all evening. I've got romance on the brain all right! Spring just does something to you inside. I think about John so much that sometimes I think I'll go crazy. Is it my imagination or am I really falling? It's very hard to tell at this age. If I don't find out tomorrow night, I'll have a nervous breakdown or something. He needs to say something to me to let me know of his feelings for me. I can't just keep guessing. I know I sound dramatic, but I need to know.

Tuesday, April 18, 1939 My Nineteenth Birthday

Well here I am one year older – 19 years old. It doesn't seem possible. Right now I'm going to vow that I get everything out of this year that I can.

Beside my stunning cigarette case I got a white blouse, a pair of pink silk panties, bath powder, a darling necklace from Aunt Milly and some toilet water from Bee.

Dad mixed some great sidecars and Mother made a perfect cheese tray. I love having my birthday in spring; my slogan - *New beginnings, New Year, New life.*

I pray it is exciting and that I make no mistakes. I'm going to make a plan and stick to it. I told the girls tonight that since this is my last teen year I'm going to have fun all year, but I'm going to be careful about it.

Sunday, April 23, 1939

Warm spring day! I've been thinking a lot about John again. You know he doesn't seem human sometimes. He's utterly strange. He's from a different world sort of. That's why I can't get next to him. He has a certain quality that isn't normal. Oh, well he's fascinating all the same.

I lay in the dark and listened to the Ford Symphony. They played Handles *Largo and Korsekof Spanish Danes*. It was beautiful and soothing.

Friday, April 28, 1939

I am so filled with emotion I can hardly write. I have just seen *Wuthering Heights*. No movie has ever been made in Hollywood as fine as this one. The movie has caught the spirit of the wild desolate moors and also the primitive Cathie and dark mysterious Heathcliff. There can be no love more perfect than theirs. I know I shan't be able to sleep tonight. That eerie atmosphere is with me and shall stay with me forever. Theirs was not a simple love, it was wrought with emotions, good and bad. Their love was a love that would endure past this earthy plain. Death could not separate them. If anything, it united them. I'm going to see that picture as many times as I can. Mother went with me too – she was spellbound.

I'm not sure if Laura should see it. It is so intense. P.S. Chuck called up while I was gone. Hmmm?

Sunday, April 30, 1939

I stayed in most of the day reading *Wuthering Heights*. Heathcliff is certainly a terrible character in the book. The critics are unanimous about raving about the movie. Who could possibly find fault with it?

I keep thinking about how brooding and romantic Lawrence Olivier is. He reminds me a bit of John. There is intensity to a man like that. He loves Cathie with such power and strength it takes your breath away. Lying in bed at night and thinking of him makes me shudder with desire.

The New York World's Fair opened this afternoon. The opening ceremonies were broadcast. They said they are expecting over 200,000 people to attend. It was such fun listening to how exciting it is there. They are having the president speak over a television. It's a box, like a radio, but you can actually see the person who is speaking. It all sounds utterly amazing! The Fair is based on the future. Their slogan is "Dawn of a New Day."

When are my exciting, new days going to begin?

Saturday, May 6, 1939

I woke up quite early this morning which is not what I expected after last night. Being on the bus all day yesterday and settling into the KDR (Kappa Delta Rho) house on campus I thought I'd be tired but I had scads of energy. I have my own room which is thrilling to be on my own.

Quite a few stayed up all night last night. Some slept with their date – in fact most of them did. I wandered all over campus with my friend Jack. His father went to school with Dad. It was so nice of him to invite me here. Colgate is such a beautiful college. Oh how I wish Dad would have allowed me to attend a real college instead of secretarial school. I think he underestimates me.

It was a gorgeous day today. We met a couple of guys Jack knows, and we started drinking at 4:00 p.m., had supper, went for a ride in a maroon convertible, came back to KDR and started to drink again at 11:00 p.m. What a brawl! I never drank so much scotch in my life. I can't remember how much I drank to be honest about it.

Sunday, May 7, 1939

What a hangover I had this morning. However, I recovered with my old standby – tomato juice and toast – that fixed me up. Our house was the weirdest on campus. It may be on Social Pen next year. A bedroom door was bashed in; not certain what was going on there. A window in the ping pong room was broken too. A lot of drunks threw bottles at passing cars. So many glasses were broken last night that there weren't enough to go around at lunch. Some place! Country Club Colgate!

One of Jack's friends took me to Syracuse to get my train. It was swell buying my ticket all alone and getting a porter to help me with my bags. I felt like Barbara Stanwyck. Then I had a swell dinner and a sidecar. I got into Buffalo at 9:10 p.m. Mother and Dad were plenty glad to see me. And was I glad to be home and sleeping in my own dear bed. I simply fell into it. Mother made me a cup of hot tea and brought it up with a biscuit. Oh how delicious it tasted. She sat at the edge of my bed and asked me if I enjoyed myself and to tell her all about it. I was dead on my feet but I gave her the run down. She was plenty concerned when I told her the amount of drinking that went on. I didn't tell her that I was keeping up with them all.

The darling let me sleep as long as I wanted to; boy did I need it!

Thursday, May 11, 1939

Well, I earned my first money today – Ginger paid me $5.00 for ten French lessons. She's going to take more too so that will make everything swell. I'll have money of my own. I went to the movies with Bee tonight. We saw Irene Dunne and Charles Boyer in *Love Affair.* It was very sophisticated and quite sad. There was a part where Irene met Charles's grandmother in her private little world where she lived over the sea, and she had her own lovely garden and chapel where she prayed and meditated every day. It was breathtaking.

Afterwards we had sandwiches and a milkshake at Holmes. My! It was quite refreshing and different after my hectic weekend.

As I went to bed tonight I realize I will have to start making some decisions about my path in life. I have to take charge.

Wednesday, May 17, 1939

Miss MacDonald, the speech teacher at school, told me that I had the makings of a very beautiful voice, that I have what all actors and actresses want to have – a low rich tone. I'm thrilled to death of course and I hope that my voice will get me somewhere. Wouldn't it be grand if I became an actress in Hollywood! Who knows!

I heard some gorgeous symphony music tonight. I am so lucky to have a radio in my bedroom. The symphony was perfectly in tune with my soul.

Saturday, May 20, 1939

I lay in bed this morning and listened to the Cincinnati Conservatory orchestra playing Tchaikovsky's *Romeo and Juliet.* I nearly went nuts. The music simply swept me away to another world.

There are plenty of blooms on all of our lilac bushes. I adore having my window open with that seductive fragrance drifting in as I lay here listening to such beautiful music. The music and fragrance simply fill my room.

I love being in my room at this moment in time. I am relishing it.

Monday, May 22, 1939

Sort of a misty, rainy morning. The trees and grass are wet and moist, a really beautiful day of its kind. It held the atmosphere of London and made me want to walk forever. Of course reality called in the name of school.

The more I go through life the more increasingly apparent it becomes that there are people who have such small souls – who never reach out and touch the sublime – who only believe in the concrete things – materialism is the word for it. I absolutely pity those people who live in such a narrow world.

Saturday, June 10, 1939

I lay in bed this morning and listened to the broadcast of the arrival of their majesties King George and Queen Elizabeth in New York City. It was very inspiring, and my eyes filled when the band played *God Save the King*, and the 21-gun salute was fine. It certainly is a great historic event. The whole U.S. is in love with the Queen.

I went downtown this afternoon and bought a darling new print dress, princess style. I got a white turban with a blue veil and a compact of which I was badly in need. I love the way everything goes so well together. I truly believe it's a Joan Crawford look for sure. I've also been working on my eyebrows looking like hers. She has a lovely arch to her brows that make her appear rather penetrating.

I did a rather funny thing today. I skipped down the street. I saw some children playing and they were laughing and skipping. So I decided to revert to my childhood for just a moment. It was great fun. It goes along with my plan to be a bit of a kid this year since it will be my last year as a teenager.

I could smell freshly mown grass and it was such a touch of summer. Everything is so green in our neighborhood. This is going to be such a fun summer. I have to get to the library and make a list for my summer reading. Miss Kelly is so good at helping me find just the right book. She knows my taste.

I had two ice cream cones today. You can't do that when you're 20.

Sunday, June 11, 1939

I wore my new dress. It looks perfectly stunning. Alas! No John, Don or Chuck to see me in it. Funny, I haven't seen much of John lately. The whole jobless thing with his father probably plays a role. I listened to a wonderful program this afternoon made up of all the English actors and actresses in honor of King George and Queen Elizabeth. Gertrude Lawrence was Mistress of Ceremonies. My heart did acrobats when Lawrence Olivier did a part from Shakespeare's "Henry IV." At the end George M. Cohan toasted their British Majesties and Cedric Hardwicke toasted President and Mrs. Roosevelt. Then they sang *God Save the King*. I was all goose pimples.

Saturday, June, 17, 1939

Bee and I went to Crystal Beach and rode most of the amusement rides. The sights, sounds and smells of an amusement park are a wonderful part of it all. It's like nothing else. People are having such a grand time together. It's all about fun and being carefree and adventurous. I ate way too much hot dogs, candy suckers, popcorn, cotton candy and soda.

I thought of Don several times tonight as I lay in bed, window open and the lovely passionate fragrance of the last vestiges of lilacs filling my room. Oh how I love to love!

Sunday, June 18, 1939

Margaret and I went to see *Wuthering Heights* again. It was grand seeing Margaret again. I haven't seen her in ages. We had a lot of catching up to do. She's really enjoying nursing school. I understand there are many very attractive doctors just ripe for the meeting. Maybe she can introduce me to some. Doctors know so much about the human anatomy, that's certainly a plus. As the movie came on the screen my heart was beating in anticipation. I enjoyed it just as much as I did the first time I saw it. It's hard to believe that a man like Lawrence Olivier exists! It made me think of John and wonder what he has been up to.

It was grand when I came home because Tommy was sitting there waiting for me. He asked me if I would like to see *Dark Victory* and of course I said yes. It was wonderful, but I didn't cry though.

Don was here while I was out, just as I suspected he would be. He even asked who I was out with. A little wondering on his part can go a long way. Then Chuck called before I went to bed and asked me if I'd like to go golfing. How wonderful! My cup runneth over!

Thursday, June 22, 1939

I got up at quarter after six. Chuck didn't get here until 7:30. It gave me time to make some coffee and have breakfast. Mrs. Brown sent some of her famous cinnamon rolls over, and I had scrambled eggs with them and a couple of pieces of bacon. I have to keep my strength up for a strenuous day of golf so I need a hearty breakfast.

Playing golf with Chuck was such fun. My game has improved since last time I played, but that isn't saying much. It's all about having fun, and I certainly enjoyed myself. Chuck plays very well. We came home and had lunch and he stayed all afternoon. He seems to feel the same way about me.

Minutes after Chuck left to go to work Don showed up! He stayed until 11:00 o'clock. He was in a perfect mood and very nice to me. It started to rain very hard – we had all of the lights out. There was lightning, thunder and everything. The intense rain pattering outside was so cozy, quite a perfect picture.

Monday, June 26, 1939

Don was over early this morning. He wanted me to suggest something for his mother's birthday present just like he did last year. I suggested some lovely toilet water and a heartfelt card.

I went to an old friend's wedding this afternoon. I knew her in grade school, and we happened to bump into each other not long ago. How very sweet of Julie to invite me like that, but she is so young, just my age. She wore a darling cream colored suit and a little hat with a veil. She looked so delicate. I hope her new husband, Ralph, will be gentle with her tonight.

I went to see *Wuthering Heights* for the fifth time with Bee. Bee never says no. She's such a good and faithful friend. Everyone should have a friend like Bee.

Chuck called up tonight. He is beyond me. Imagine apologizing for not being over because of his cousin being in town. Well, anyway, devotion like that is very gratifying.

Thursday, June 27, 1939

It's Dada's 83rd birthday. I gave her "Evening in Paris" powder and perfume. She adored it. She received lots of flowers and birthday cards. Mother made a delicious meal, a pasta dish that she found in a cookbook of Dada's. It was a white cream sauce with mushrooms and garlic and we had a salad with early big red tomatoes from our garden. We put the radio on and listened to some beautiful symphony music. She stayed up later than usual, and we sat out on the side porch and had a glass of red wine. You could hear the crickets and the kids playing way past their bed time. It was one of those nights when the air is warm but not too hot. It was so nice having the three generations of women enjoying a beautiful summer night. Dad had gone to bed early. I do so hope I have a daughter. I think I'll call her Elizabeth after the Queen.

Wednesday, June 28, 1939

Mrs. Graney had a beautiful luncheon for Mary Louise, not a close friend but a dear girl. Our mothers grew up together. It was held at the Park Club another club I wish we belonged to. What a splendid day! We sat out on the terrace and had a champagne toast wishing Mary Louise a sunny day on her wedding and many blessings for her future. Mother said that when I get married I will be able to choose from either the Saturn Club or the Park Club for my reception. I feel it would depend on what time of year I get married.

Chuck, Don and Bee were over this afternoon. Roughhousing times were a part of the day. It's always exciting when Chuck and Don are together. They both try to earn my favor. Bee gets annoyed sometimes.

Mother and I were in the attic this morning. It was like a steam bath up there. She was looking for her wedding dress. She wants to see what she can do with it for me. It's very dated, and I delicately explained that it would be a great deal of work for something I wouldn't wear.

Tuesday, July 4, 1939

This has been the hottest day so far this summer. I slept in the nude. What a luscious feeling sleeping against cool, crisp sheets. Laura brought the kittens over and we hid them in the cellar from Dad. The firecrackers are too loud on their street, and all the noise frightens them.

I went swimming with Bee and Ruth today. We drove to Crystal Beach. What a time we had. We were sunbathing on the beach then found a small secluded spot to sunbathe nude. Oh that sun on our skin felt dreamy. We had to scurry to put our suits back on when we heard boys approaching. This will be another nightie-less night for me.

I love that feeling after you have been swimming all day, that waterlogged, tired and dreamy state of mind.

I can't wait for my head to hit the pillow tonight. As I'm writing this I'm so tired I could fall asleep at my dressing table.

Friday, July 7, 1939

I bought a new hat today. There were so many choices. It was so difficult making up my mind.

Chuck was over tonight. He seems to be crazy about me. He and I were sitting on the side porch. We could hear the music of summer, the crickets chirping, children playing hide and seek and the far-off sound of a train whistle. Then he kissed me and asked me to go steady. Of course I refused. He said I'm the only girl he ever really wanted. It all sounds wonderful, but I can't lead him on or I'll get into a jam.

That train whistle haunted me.

Saturday, July 8, 1939

I went to a birthday luncheon at Cherry Hill for Janet Stevens. She's been playing golf with me lately. It was swell of her to invite me since we are fairly new friends. She's a real beauty too, a Jean Harlow look-alike. Her mother looks as beautiful as she does.

So funny, I ran into Don and Chuck playing golf. They were both so attentive. Of course I enjoy it immensely. Chuck says Don and I are going steady and that he's going to put it in the Buffalo News Listening Post. I'm so glad that Janet wasn't around when I was with the boys. She's tough competition.

I'm thrilled about everything!

Friday, July 14, 1939

Dear Diary: You are the only one I can tell. Somehow I know that Don is the only person I'll ever care for. It will probably be years before anything will come of the way I feel. I've got to keep everything from him or I haven't a chance. That's going to be hard acting nonchalant about things, going nuts while he's back at Duke. I pray right now for my dreams to come true no matter how long it takes.

Don came over this afternoon. Thump! Thump!

Sunday, July 16, 1939

We had an uproarious time at dinner. Uncle George and Uncle Charlie were teasing Mother. It was one laugh after another. I'm certainly glad that I don't have brothers, the way Mother's treat her sometimes. She's one who can handle it though. I'm too sensitive.

In the evening we all went over to Aunt Milly and Uncle George's for an elegant dinner. We laughed all evening. How wonderful our family is. We may have a small family, but we have large hearts.

Dad got home from Detroit. I always miss him so when he's not home. He had a marvelous time as usual. He seems to enjoy being on the road sometimes. He always comes home with a kick in his step.

I'm still head-over-heals in love with Don. My heart flutters terribly whenever I think about him. Maybe I only think I am. But I guess I ought to know. After all I'm 19 years old. If I don't know now I never will. What is it that holds me back?

Tuesday, July 25, 1939

Chuck was over all afternoon. He made beautiful love to me, and it's very hard to keep from being stirred. I really feel that he is sincere.

I took a golf lesson with Bee and we played nine holes afterward. I'm doing really well.

When I got home around 10:00 p.m. and Don and Chuck were over all dressed fit to kill.

We had a little rye at our house and then we went to Mann's. I only had two beers but Don and Chuck drank quite a bit. Don certainly acts different after he's had a few drinks. Chuck was smooth to me all the way home. I'm crazy about them both!

Wednesday, July 26, 1939

Mother and I went downtown, and I bought a new green print dress; Mother bought a coat. Bee was over this afternoon and loved our purchases.

In the evening Nan Thompson and I went to the concert at the art gallery. When we came out, and I started to drive away I got a flat tire. This musician from the orchestra offered to help me and to drive me to a telephone. I called Dad of course. The musician started to fix the tire when a brown coupe came in sight and out of it jumped Dad, Don and Chuck to the rescue of fair lady. Chuck fixed the tire. He's an expert. Don and I were both getting a big kick out of it.

Dad took us to Coles for a beer. Boy was I hungry. We had sandwiches, and Bee and I talked non-stop about how beautiful the music was.

Friday, July 28, 1939

Still hot! Ruth, Margaret, Don and I played bridge. Chuck came over and we had a riot. Don took the girls home then came back of course. I know he didn't want me to be alone with Chuck very long. They both helped me with the dishes. Somehow I have a hunch that Chuck suspects I like Don a great deal. I can't hide the look in my eyes I guess. All I know is that I never wanted anyone as much as I want Don; if he would only kiss me. I have forgotten what his kisses are like.

I took an ice bath before I went to bed. I certainly needed it.

Saturday, July 29, 1939

Rain at last! Intermittently all day. I'm reading *Guns of Burgoyne*. It is an excellent book. Bee is leaving Monday for New York. She's looking into schools. She wants to go into research.

Don came over tonight before he went to his poker game. He looked smooth and had a new hat he was very anxious for me to see. He's just a little boy at heart! He is always teasing me about going steady with Chuck. I guess that's a defense. If he only knew what my heart truly felt, he wouldn't worry about Chuck.

Monday, July 31, 1939

Nan and I went to see *The Man in The Iron Mask*. It was super. What an awful thought, having an iron mask on your face for years. I hope I don't have nightmares tonight.

I came home and took a nap. I was so tired from last night. Imagine Don kissing me in his car six times. I was completely overwhelmed. His technique is so reserved, so different from Chuck's.

Saturday, August 5, 1939

I had some girls over tonight. We played bridge and listened to the radio. Chuck and Don came and brought beer with them as usual. After my guests went home I went to Coles with Don and Chuck. Some of Chuck's friends on his baseball team asked him over to join them for a drink. I know he didn't want to leave Don and me alone, but his friends didn't leave him much of a choice.

I was thinking how swell it was turning out for me, stealing some alone time with Don, when out of nowhere he dropped a bombshell on me. He seemed worried all night about something. Then he told me in all seriousness that he is engaged! He said it was some girl named Mary Ruth down in Virginia!

How can he be kissing me all the time and be engaged!! What sort of man is he? I don't get it.

I better start rethinking things. Mother did say that there are a lot of fish in the sea. I have to put my pole in the water.

Wednesday, August 9, 1939

What a night! Don told me that he had a date with Barbara Shanley the other night. He's dating and he's engaged!? Again, I don't get it.

Bee sent me a coral necklace from the Fair in New York. She said it's thrilling there and that she misses me terribly. I've been too busy to notice she's gone.

I had a riotous time here tonight. We were ravenous all of the sudden and raided Mother's pantry and Dad's bar. We had cocktails, all the salami in the house, two loaves of Mother's homemade bread, apple pie, olives, crackers, etc.

Mitch and Don got in a fight in our backyard. Of course they had been drinking too much. I don't even know what the fight was about. Don's tongue was bleeding. Chuck wouldn't leave the house until Don did – he won't let me be alone with him. Things are so involved. I don't know what end is up!

With all of the food and half of Dad's bar in their stomachs I don't understand how they could even stand up.

Friday, August 11, 1939

So now Don is telling me that he is "practically" engaged to Mary Ruth and that he doubted that it would ever materialize because she lives so far way. I'm glad but still bewildered. Marriage is such an important step to take in life. You are saying that you want to spend the rest of your days with that one person. He seems so casual about it all.

I'm reading *The Rains Came* by Louis Bromfield. It's very good. Ruth came over and we talked about sex. I shared the book that Tommy gave me on birth control. She was enthralled. There are still many questions that won't be answered in any book that I know of or would be able to get my hands on. Why does it all have to be such a mystery?

Saturday, August 12, 1939

The rain started around six o'clock and kept up all evening long, a very appropriate setting in which to read *The Rains Came*. I sat out on the side porch with an ice tea reading. This is one of the simple pleasures I enjoy most. It smells so good too. I put my book down and closed my eyes and allowed myself to daydream. Everyone should daydream.

Chuck arrived dressed flawlessly and looking as handsome as any woman could want. We went for a long ride in the rain. He had brought a small basket with beer and pretzels his mother made, so warm and delicious. We sat in the car with the pitter-patter of rain coming down on the car roof. How cozy and warm. We talked about relationships and how different they are nowadays. Parents today don't seem to have any passion left in them. It all seems to have dried up.

Although Chuck is devastating I shouldn't let him make love to me because always there is that relentless shadow of Don over me all of the time. I can't get rid of it. I keep seeing his face all of the time. He haunts me.

Monday, August 14, 1939

I bought the most darling shorts today, bright yellow with an orange belt. I have a shirt to match it. I also have a yellow ribbon I want to wear in my hair. It was a quick shopping trip. It seems that I am so busy lately. My calendar is always filled.

Nan and I went to the movies to see *Brother Rat* when all of the sudden we got into a terrible car accident on Delaware Ave. Nan had to bang into a tree to avoid hitting the other car. She was badly hurt but saved my life. Her face was all blood. I couldn't get out of the car because my leg hurt so and was pinned inside. People did get me free and laid me out on the ground, then the ambulance came and got both of us. It was a terrifying scene.

They fixed my leg up at the hospital. Nan had to be taken to surgery. Mother and Dad came and got me, and I came home and went to bed. The doctor gave me something to help me sleep.

Tuesday, August 15, 1939

I ached all over this morning. I had to see Dr. Kenewell so he could put a new bandage on my leg. I stopped at Millard Fillmore Hospital to see Nan but only family was allowed to visit. She lost ten teeth, and her lower lip is hacked to pieces. Dr. Wakefield operated on her jaw last night. The awful thing about the accident is that the other car that caused it got away.

Chuck has been at my side constantly.

Thursday, August 17, 1939

Mr. Hurd from American Mutual Insurance Co. took me downtown to be examined for the company policy. I can walk perfectly well except for walking up and down stairs. That will take a while.

Carol came over to stay all night. She is so worried about me. What a wonderful cousin she is. Of course Laura is equally worried, but too many overnight visitors may be too much for me. They are better than sisters. Chuck and Don came and the four of us had a swell time together. Carol talked to Don and found out a lot of stuff for me. He told her he likes me best. I hope that means over Mary Ruth. If he likes me best, why is he considering marrying her?

Chuck likes me so. I do adore him, but it's so much better for me to like Don because Chuck and I can never marry. I hope I find my way out of this mess.

Tuesday, August 22, 1939

I went downtown and experienced the thrill of a lifetime! I've got a new fur coat – the most beautiful mink-dyed muskrat I've ever seen.

I took a golf lesson and was lousy. I really have to concentrate more on my swing. Dad is such a great golfer. I know he can give me some tips.

Uncle George got me a job in a swell real estate office. I start tomorrow at 11:00 a.m. My boss is Mr. Geischer. I'm petrified and awfully excited. I hope I make good. Earning my own money will be a thrill. Two exciting events in one day; I need some nerve tablets.

Wednesday, August 23, 1939

Fifteen dollars a week! And am I thrilled! Mr. Geischer is swell and so is his son. I have to keep the books. Bud (the son) is helping me until I get used to it. I have a Royal typewriter and naturally feel at home. I simply love this job. I feel as though I am embarking on a true career, not just working at something that doesn't hold my interest. I'm not sure if I would enjoy being a realtor all my life, but it's a grand start.

Chuck was over tonight. We snuggled in the green chair, and he looked deep into my blue eyes and told me that when he heard I was in an accident his heart sank so deeply he thought he would die. He told me right then and there that he was in love with me. Honestly that makes it all the harder. I keep thinking about Don. I want him so. If he could only see me with Chuck I'm sure it would stir his jealous tendencies. I can't help it though: I'm only a woman.

Friday, August, 25, 1939

I'm more crazy about my job each day. I got my first paycheck $7.50 for half a week. Do I feel important!

The war crisis in Europe is terrific. Loads of Americans are evacuating Europe. The Russian – Germany part sure made fireworks. The Poles are determined to fight. The Americans will probably be dragged into it in time if there is a war. Then life just won't be worth living!

Sunday, August 27, 1939

Mother altered my black dress with a new gold neckline. It looks stunning. Mother and I went next door to the Browns to play bridge. We won handily. It's such a hot evening; too hot for Mrs. Brown to bake anything. Rats!

The war crisis will reach its climax tomorrow morning when Neville Chamberlain goes back to Germany with Britain's' answer. The world will be praying tonight.

I haven't been praying for anything lately – just letting things work out for themselves including Don.

Wednesday, August 30, 1939

I had quite a busy day at the office. Bud is a riot. We have a swell time talking when his dad isn't in the office. Big surprise when I got home. The Browns have a stunning new Pontiac Eight Coupe- green with white wall tires and a radio. It's perfectly super.

I haven't heard from Don lately. I hope I see him before he goes back to Duke. I wonder if I can take it.

Friday, September 1, 1939

Europe is ablaze! Germany bombed three Polish cities and now they are at war. England will probably be in it by tomorrow night. We eventually will get in it, and the future of our generation will be nil!

Still nothing from Don. What's going on?

Sunday, September 3, 1939

This is a fateful day in the lives of all of us. England and France both declared themselves in a state of war with Germany. Bulletins have come in all day. Radio programs are interrupted all the time, and then there are loads of transmitted broadcasts. King George and President Roosevelt both spoke to their people.

Some ships carrying 1,400 passengers were torpedoed by Germany. How I hope we can keep out of it.

Don, Dad, Mother and I played bridge. We had the radio on while we played. It was so difficult trying to concentrate. I couldn't help staring at Don's beautiful, young face. Will he be wearing a uniform soon? Will Chuck? Will John? Don stayed until 2:30. He fell asleep on the davenport. He just wanted to be with us I think.

Tuesday, September 5, 1939

Bud at work and I had a confidential talk about the problems of youth. I really got some good points from a person who knows.

Mr. Brown is in the hospital and is going to be operated on for kidney stones.

Don, Mother, Dad and I played bridge tonight. Chuck was here too, and the boys put away four quarts of beer. We had a riot of a time. Mother was the life of the party. I only had two glasses of beer because I'm a working gal.

Dad went to bed early as he has a big day tomorrow. We had to make sure to keep it down to a dull roar. It was not so easy to do since we were all having such a good time.

Wednesday, September 6, 1939

The ware in Europe is hot! Germany is holding three fronts and is almost at Warsaw's door. As yet the British and French haven't done anything spectacular. The price of sugar here has gone up. People are buying it up. It's a very silly thing to do. The U.S. has declared its neutrality. Let's hope it works.

Mother, Bee and I went to the movies. It's the first time I've been in a month. Mother bought a large box of popcorn for all of us to share and sodas all around. I have so missed going to the movies. I love to lose myself in the story.

Wednesday, September 13, 1939

Don came over tonight and waited for me to get home from the Paul Whiteman broadcast. Chuck and Mitch came over too. How I wanted to be alone this evening. It seems as though I have very little time to myself. All of this news about the possibility of war is something I need to process. It is such a frightening time.

Chuck and Mitch left, and Don and I were alone. I felt very weary as if the windows had eyes. We sat in the sun porch, and I was really feeling one of those enchanted moments coming on, when suddenly the door opened. Mitch and Chuck walked in. Chuck said "What's the big idea?" wising around?" He pulled Don up off the summer davenport and socked him. I was petrified. Chuck stopped finally. Don's mouth was bleeding. I was a nervous wreck. Chuck and Mitch turned around and left. Don stayed. I hardly know what to say.

Thursday, September 14, 1939

All day I worried what Don must think. Chuck did a terrible thing. Jealousy is awful. I'll never forget his words. "Can I help it if I see red when I see another fellow put a hand on you?" Don said to Chuck last night, "You know I'd never lay a hand on Deborah in the way you think." Those words touched my heart.

Don promised he would come tonight to say goodbye. Well he didn't come, and I cried all evening. At 10:30 there he was standing at the door and all was right with the world. We went for a ride, and he was so adorable. He means so much to me. He kissed me goodbye very impulsively; I watched his car until it was out of sight.

As he drove away I couldn't help wondering Mary Ruth? Ginger? Myself? Or some mystery girl that none of us knows about? He certainly keeps us all guessing. And I'm not one for guessing games.

Friday, September 15, 1939

It was a terribly hot day. The boss went to New York, and it's swell with just Bud and me. I told him all about the other night's happenings. He absolutely thinks I should give Chuck the gate. I hope he never comes to my house again. I think I made it plain how I feel about Don.

All day I've thought about Don. I'll never forget last night. To think it will be December before I see him again. It's so unfair the way school has to come between us.

The way I always like to remember the two of us is when we were running up the front walk in the night, his hand in mine, I in my satin housecoat and silver slippers shining in the moonlight and Don holding a bag of beer bottles.

Tuesday, September 19, 1939

Very slow day at the office. Bee came over, and we talked up in my bedroom. She is my best friend. She thinks I should focus on my future and try to forget boys for a while. That's not an option.

Chuck came over, and Dad went to the door and sort of told him how things stood. He said that in life a man has to learn how to control his anger. He also told him that I was just as mad as ever and that he himself was greatly disappointed in Chuck and his behavior. Chuck said thank you sir and walked away.

I pulled back the curtain in the living room, and I could see him slowly walk down the steps with the weight of the world on his shoulders. I still can't feel right about it. Somehow I'll have to talk to Chuck because I can't bear being mad at anyone, especially in these uncertain times.

As I go to bed tonight I pray this Chuck affair will turn out all right. How can I be angry at someone who loves me such much that he was willing to fight for me. I have to be fair about this. Chuck deserves his day in court.

Wednesday, September 20, 1939

Mr. Geischer got back this afternoon. I knew there would be some work to do. When I have nothing to do, I think and think and think about Chuck. Oh Lord, how will it end? I can't kid myself. I do care for him. I do miss him so.

Mother went downtown and bought me a beautiful plaid skirt and white cardigan sweater. Also a moss green dress and stockings; of course I'm going to pay for them out of my paycheck. That feels good.

Ruth, Bee and I went to see a John Hodiak movie. He can put his shoes under my bed anytime!

Thursday, September 21, 1939

I had lunch with Ann Clark. She's working at the First National Bank a block away from me. She's doing well, and she said that she will be getting married next month. She apologized for not being able to invite me to the ceremony as her husband to be is "joining up," and he'll be shipping out soon. There really is no time to plan a real wedding. They will be getting married in her parent's living room.

The war is really terrific now. Poland is almost conquered. Germany and Russia are doing pretty well for themselves! I suppose we'll have to get in eventually to stop them. Oh for a pot shot at Hitler's mustache!

I bought a Viking blue dress at the Sample Shop. It has the zipper down the front and is absolutely darling. I went over to see Carol and Laura's new bedroom. They moved to a new house on Voorhees. It's a beautiful home.

Saturday, September 23, 1939

Nan and I went to the movies to see *The Rains Came*. It was marvelous and followed the book perfectly. Nan's face breaks my heart; she still has scars from the accident. I thought the surgeon would have been able to do a better job than that. Some people were staring at her when we walked into the theater.

Dada said Chuck stopped by and just sat in his car out front. She noticed him through the window. I sure wish I'd been home. I've been thinking of nothing else this past week

They played lovely romantic music on the radio tonight. I thought of Chuck, not Don.

Is this the part of the movie where I say to hell with religious division and conventions to run off with the boy next door and live happily ever after?

Sunday, September 24, 1939

I wore my new blue dress – the color matches my mood. I think I have a hat to go with it somewhere.

The Irwins were over for supper and the evening as well. I've been very preoccupied all day. I have been thinking of Chuck all the time. I just can't help myself. He is a memory I can't wipe out with nonchalance. I hope so much that he's thinking of me. I guess what I want most of all is to be loved!

Wednesday, September 27, 1939

It rained all day. Work is perfect. I hope it keeps up that way. My bedroom is all papered. It looks beautiful. It goes well with my furniture.

Nothing is happening in my private life, and that is the most important to me.

Warsaw surrendered to the Nazis today. England and France are still pounding away at Germany.

Thursday, September 28, 1939

My bedroom has new curtains to match my bedspread. Gorgeous is the word. Mother and I had to hunt and hunt for lilac wallpaper. I'm so pleased that we finally found some. It's beautiful. I feel as though I'm sleeping in a garden filled with lilac bushes. What a dream room I have.

Oh will Christmas never come?! I just want to see all the kids again; wine in our silver decanter, candles on the table and the general magical atmosphere that goes with the most perfect holiday.

I haven't heard a word from Chuck. I'm practically at my wits end. I'm reading *Grapes of Wrath*. It's heartbreaking. This is not the best book to be reading with the mood I'm in already.

Saturday, September 30, 1939

I went to the show with Bee and saw *The Women* adapted from the famous stage play. It was a riot and showed our sex in its true light. Norma Shearer was marvelous as she always is. She was so strong and elegant, just the way I want to be. I cried a lot in the sad scenes. It was so fascinating not having any men in the movie at all, not one.

I now have $15.00 in the bank. I didn't buy anything downtown. I'll be Christmas shopping soon enough.

They played all the romantic and nostalgic songs tonight. I nearly went nuts when they played *Lamp is Low*. Chuck used to sing it to me. *I'll Remember* is my favorite song – it brings back memories of Chuck and me together. Oh! What have I done to that dear boy!

Sunday, October 1, 1939

I went to church for the first time since May. It was very relaxing but I always meditate on the one person who's been on my mind for two weeks. Oh God please bring him back to me. I can't go on like this. Just to hear the sound of his voice, to see the look in his eyes, to feel his lips on mine. My heart is reeling my love and I don't care. It's the only way to live.

He wasn't afraid to profess his love for me. He wasn't afraid to fight for me. When I was injured, who was the first person to show up? Chuck.

I wore my new brown hat and Aunt Milly's stunning tweed sports coat. I looked as if I stepped out of Vogue. I'd give anything to have that coat.

I wonder what it would be like to be a model or an actress. Poor Nan, she could have been a model. She was such a pretty girl. I do hope she gets her looks back eventually.

Monday, October 2, 1939

Bee was over tonight. We spent the whole evening trying to think how to tell Chuck that I forgive him. I've got to see him before October 12 so we can have our date on that night, our anniversary of sorts. All I can think of is the cute things he used to do. He made such beautiful love to me. I measure every other kiss to his. Oh, Chuck darling, please come back!!

Tuesday, October 3, 1939

I got my two tickets for Katherine Cornell in *No Time for Comedy*. I'm taking Mother out. $1.65 seats, fourth row in the balcony.

Bee and I beat Mother and Dad at bridge tonight. It was a warm evening for October, a gentle breeze outside, a touch of burning leaves in the air. I just love October. The phone rang and Mother answered it. There wasn't a sound and then a clicking noise. I wonder if it could have been Chuck. I do hope so. Every time the phone rings I jump a mile. Let's hope it's he one of these nights.

Thursday, October 5, 1939

Some friends of Martha Linden are starting a bridge club, and Nan and I are both in it. Nan is looking much better. It's amazing what carefully applied make-up can do.

The first meeting was tonight at Anne Cook's. We had a grand time. I met two people I haven't seen in ages – Dixie Badger and Jean Campbell – way back from my summer at Long Beach when I was 13 years old.

Monday, October 9, 1939

I worked all day today trying to find a $2.00 difference. At quarter to four I found the difference. It was Bud's mistake. I was thrilled. So pleased it wasn't mine.

Bee was down tonight. She has a job as flower hostess at Millard Fillmore Hospital. I think it's wonderful.

At last I think I shall take matters into my own hands. I wrote a note to Chuck which I shall post in the morning. I pray to God that he meets me on Thursday night in our spot.

Tuesday, October 10, 1939

Well, I mailed the letter. Thank God it's off my mind. If he doesn't come Thursday night I'll know that he wants to forget me, so either way it will be okay.

It rained all day. I love it especially when the leaves are falling, as they are now.

I went to the show with Ruth. We saw the French film *Lucretia Borgia*. It was excellent and my first foreign film.

Thursday October 12, 1939

Chuck came as I hoped so much he would – looking as attractive as ever. We walked Bee home. Then we went over to the fountain. Chuck doesn't like Don at all. He didn't seem to regret hitting him very much. He talked a lot about the foreign situation and the future. He was so mature and serious in his tone. These are very serious times of course, but it was so out of character for Chuck to at this way.

He never seemed so likable and desirable to me before. He said if he had a nickel for every time he's thought of me in the past two weeks he could buy a new Packard. He told me he was in love with me. I am, but not completely, with him. It's oh so good to be with him again and in his arms. I'll have to help him square things with Dad very soon.

Friday, October 13, 1939

I think of Chuck all the time. Life is so queer. Here all the time I thought I was in love with Don and now I hardly think about him at all.

Mother, Bee and I went to the movies. We saw *The Wizard of Oz*. What an unusual movie! It was excellent. What color, so beautiful! And that Judy Garland is just a doll. What a voice she has. I thought it was so clever how they went from black and white to color. What a shock for the senses!

It's rather cold today. I'm fully prepared for winter with my fur coat and snow shoes.

Thursday, October 19, 1939

Every day at the office is a riot. Bud teases me beyond words of expression. Gee! I'm so lucky to have a job that's so much fun.

Bridge club is at my house tonight. Everyone arrived on time. I showed all the girls my fur coat. It was a sensation!

I can't understand why I haven't heard from Chuck. He has been, and probably always will be, my big romance. I wonder if I will ever meet anyone else. Who knows?

Saturday, October 21, 1939

Well, Mother, Dad and I had our long planned good time today. We went shopping first. I have joined the literary guild.

Katherine Cornell in *No Time for Comedy* was too wonderful for words to describe. She is fascinating and such an actress! Francis Lederer was devastating. He is so dark, handsome and suave. I hope I dream about him tonight. The legitimate stage really is tops.

After the show we were on top of the world. We went to Laube's Old Spain for a lobster dinner; cocktails too. We kept on going and went to the movies to see Leslie Howard in *Intermezzo* which was quite exquisite. I have $5.00 left from my pay envelope. What a wonderful night!

Sunday, October 22, 1939

I did practically nothing all day. Chuck is still on my mind. If I don't see him this week, I'll be convinced that he doesn't give a hoot about me. I wonder sometimes if I'll ever have a steady boyfriend. I'm beginning to yearn for security. I could never go steady with Chuck because he's a Catholic and so far he's the only one who has asked me.

Tuesday, October 24, 1939

I finished *Twenty Years After* at work. What a slow day it was.

Bee was over tonight, and we played bridge with Mother and Dad. We got licked as usual.

The war is still on in Europe. Germany seized a United States freighter today. That really sounds bad. Any more tricks like that and we'll be in it for sure.

This is without a doubt the loveliest October I've ever seen. Each day is a shining jewel with clear blue skies and scarlet red autumn leaves. Romance is in the air, but none for me. I long for Chuck's arms so much. I wonder if he will always have such an impression on me.

Wednesday, October 25, 1939

I had a long talk with Nan on the phone. She is such a strong young woman. I'm so proud of her and the way she has handled her appearance. She has done a wonderful job with make-up, but the scars are still there and they are rather deep. The dentist did a great job on her teeth. She'll do well in life with her attitude.

Shortly after she called wonder of wonders – Chuck called me. I had about a half an hour conversation with him. He's called Bee but she hasn't been home, also he called here but Dad answered the phone, and Chuck just couldn't muster the courage at that point to speak to him.

I was so glad to hear his voice. I told him how I wished we could relive those days when I was a senior at Bennett and I'd find him waiting for me each day when I got home. We did some reminiscing, all very sentimental underneath. You can never call time back again.

Saturday, October 28, 1939

I went downtown with Mother. I spent money like a drunken sailor. I bought some darling silver slippers $3.95. I got high heeled suede pumps and a wine colored dress, a blue satin blouse, two books, cologne and bath salts. I'm so happy about everything.

I've got my new nightgown on right now as I sit here writing. I feel quite the elegant woman. I know there's one person who would love to see me in it.

Wednesday, November 1, 1939

We are now 60 cents out in our books at work. Bud says he'd rather try to find the mistake than eat. He's in a swell humor lately. I'm sure we'll find it. It does make me nervous. I want to be an employee that stands out. Mistakes are not in my nature. I do believe it was Bud's error.

Dada had a heart attack this afternoon. The doctor doesn't seem to think it's very serious, but Aunt Milly thinks she's had another stroke. Uncle George is worried about Mother. I wish I could help her more, but I have my job to get to.

Monday, November 6, 1939

The doctor was here this morning and said that Dada was very low – just a case of 24 to 36 hours. He said we should be thankful that she is leaving us because gangrene will set in her leg very soon. Her breathing is bad at times.

Tonight Dada is in and out of a coma. She doesn't recognize anyone except Uncle George. He talked with Dad and made funeral arrangements. We are all sitting around waiting. Mother is a wreck, and I am so tired. None of us will get very much sleep tonight.

Tuesday, November 7, 1939

I'm dead tired; my eyes are so heavy. Dada is still alive. She is hanging in with all the determination in the world. It's terrible that it is so prolonged. Gangrene is in her leg. If she doesn't pass away soon her leg will have to be removed. This waiting is awful. Mother has deep circles under her eyes.

Dada's bedroom is next to mine. She is laying in her large mahogany bed. I can hear her labored breathing now as I write at my dressing table. I so want for her to be at peace. It is raining tonight – desolate.

Wednesday, November 8, 1939 Dear Dada passed away at 4:10 a.m. this morning. Uncle George was with her when she died. In the afternoon we all went to the funeral home to see her. She looks lovely in the orchid dress that was my favorite and which I requested. The casket is quilted white There is a gorgeous bower of pink roses tied with an orchid bow on top of the casket.

The Chambers were kind enough to have the florist send them over.

It is so hard to believe that it is all over with. I am so dead tired from the whole thing. Grandmother Peters called today with her condolences. We had a long talk, she and I. I told her how much I'm going to miss Dada. She said that she will be coming for a visit soon. And then she paused for a moment and added very sweetly, "I know how close you were to Dada because she had been living with you. You are my only grandchild, and you are so very dear to me. Would you mind terribly if I asked you to call me Grammie?" You could have knocked me over with a feather. Then she told me that she has been talking to Dad about moving back to Buffalo. This was even before Dada had fallen ill. Dad has rented a lovely apartment for her not far from us. How wonderful it will be to have her so close.

It will be a bit difficult to call Grandmother Peters Grammie. When I discussed this with Dad he told me that she had wanted to ask me to call her that years ago, but she felt it might be forced. I wish she had suggested to me that I call her that years ago.

My two grandmothers are so different; different in a very good way. They have taught me so much.

Friday, November 10, 1939

Mother is out of town to visit relatives and recoup. This is a much needed break for her. I got Dad's breakfast this morning. I did a nice job of it too. I washed the dishes and made both beds before I left for work.

I went to the church for the picking of parts for the play. I am going to be the nurse. It will be fun I'm sure of it. I think it's a good idea for me to get a taste of what it would be like to have a career as an actress. It's true my part isn't a large one, but I intend on making the most of it.

Sunday, November 12, 1939

I wrote to Don last night. I told him of Dada's passing. I find myself thinking about him a great deal lately.

I saw Bette Davis in *The Old Maid.* I cried so. It was wonderful. I certainly hope that never happens to me. Mother says the way boys flock to me like moths to a flame I'll never have to worry about that. She said my only problem will be choosing the boy I like best. I think Mother leans towards Chuck, but Dad would never allow my marrying a Catholic. I don't think Mother would mind so much. I can tell she doesn't really like Don. She referred to him as a "cold fish" once. And she certainly doesn't like the fact that he said he was engaged and continued to date.

Things seem so strange around here without Dada. Sometimes I look at Mother and she has a far-off look, and I know that she's thinking of Dada and missing her. I couldn't go on without my mother.

I think I'm going to make dinner sometime this week to give her some time to herself. She could use a night off. Mother has been through so much. There is such a strange emptiness to our home now without her. She was a very strong presence.

Saturday, November 25, 1939

Margaret called. I haven't talked to her in a while. We went downtown and did some Christmas shopping. It's so beautiful – churches have their crèches out, and the city is all aglitter with decorations everywhere. The cold North wind is beginning to blow.

The unexpected happened at 11:20 p.m. Chuck called, and we had over an hour conversation. He has been plenty busy. It was so good to hear his voice. I've been thinking of him so much lately. He very kindly asked how our family was doing since Dada's passing. He's so thoughtful. I haven't heard a word from Don about it. He does seem like rather a cold fish.

Sunday, November 26, 1939

Chuck couldn't get the car tonight, so no go! I was so disappointed. Then one of those moths to a flame that Mother was talking about came over. John was at my door. I haven't seen him in quite a while. He and his friend Ray invited me over to Ray's home. His parents were there and invited me to stay for dinner. John had asked me to bring my music with me. We played the piano all evening. We had a swell time. I do like John so much, but I can't get to first base with him since he swore off necking. Why in the world he would do that I'm sure I don't know. It really is enough to provoke a woman.

Saturday, December 2, 1939

Nan, Ruth and I went to the Buffalo Shea's to see Gene Krupa and his band. He was super! Watching him beat those drums is very arousing. Tyrone Power in *Daytime Wife* was grand too.

I bought Mother some Elizabeth Arden "Night and Day" cologne for Christmas. It's delicious smelling; nothing but the best for Mother.

Sunday, December 3, 1939

John and I went bowling. We had a grand time. I have improved a great deal. I got 100! I think it's pretty okay because I'm a novice and play in high heels.

I started a new book, *Christmas Holiday*. It's very good and quite unusual, not at all what you would expect from such a title. Mother and I were alone tonight. Dad was at the club. Mother and I talked about the magic of Christmas and our childhood memories of it. Softy falling snow, sleigh rides and jingle bells, singing around the piano and the mistletoe! Oh how I love the mistletoe! Being with people you love of course is the most important part of the season.

There is a very mysterious package in Mother's bedroom.

I feel like going down and playing some Christmas music on our piano. Mother and Dad love it when I do that spur of the moment.

Thursday, December 7, 1939

Our play rehearsal was at Nan's. I called for John by request. John was swell to me all evening – even helped me with my coat. I was quite overcome.

John smokes a pipe. He looked very romantic while playing the piano. When he plays *Liebestraum* it's perfect. I do wish we could get a new piano.

Mother was baking all day today. Oh how I love the smell of homemade bread. She also made a batch of Christmas cookies. It was a little early, but she said she just had a moment and was thinking about Dada. She and Dada used to make the cookies together, and I would put the frosting on. I do miss her so.

Grammie is moving into her new apartment at the first of the year. It still seems rather funny calling her that, funny but nice.

She's going to have me over for tea soon.

Sunday, December 10, 1939

John and I talked for hours tonight after we played bridge with Mother and Dad. I really got the inside dope on him, which relieves my mind quite a bit. After we talked life over thoroughly, we talked about books, music, art and the theater. Before we realized it the time was twenty to one a.m.

Monday, December 11, 1939

I went to dinner at Laube's Old Spain and then to see Garbo in *Ninochka*. Ruth came with me. We had a lovely time. What an actress she is. Garbo is like no other presence on the screen. She moves and speaks with such strength. She is rather an intimidating figure I must say.

We took a cab to the Saturn Club and sat in the Red Room by the fire. It was rather quiet for a night in December so close to Christmas. I am always in awe of how grand and beautiful it is there especially during the holidays. Dave made a great cocktail for me; it hit me right between the eyes. Merry Christmas!

Saturday, December 16, 1939

I went downtown and took Laura with me. It was so crowded. The stores are gorgeous – so magical. I can hardly wait for Christmas. I do feel that I have been neglecting Laura. Carol and I are so much closer in age and our experiences in life mirror one another. Laura is such a sweet little spirit. I'm glad I spent the afternoon with her. I bought Mother a lovely nightie for another present. I love spoiling her.

I went home and wrapped presents and got all my cards addressed. I make sure to write a little note in each card to make it special.

John asked me over to his house. We played duets on the piano. It was too rare for words. He took me up in this room in his attic to show me his books – quite unconventional but who cares.

I have more wrapping to do. Dad brought his gifts up for Mother as he always does. He's all thumbs when it comes to wrapping a package. I love doing it for him. He bought her some lovely things this year as he always does.

Monday, December 18, 1939

My old friend Tommy asked me to the college ball on Christmas night. I'm so excited I can hardly write this. Wow! Now if I could be with Don New Year's Eve, everything would be perfect.

I went over to see Carol and Laura. It is very exciting over there. Their tree is enormous! There are presents all over the place. Gee! I can hardly wait. Life is too perfect.

Tuesday, December 19, 1939

I went downtown to look at evening dresses tonight. We went to three stores, and I couldn't find a thing. I did find a beautiful gift for Laura – a lovely strand of Richelieu Pearls. I'm so excited about the college ball and just everything all put together. Now all I've got to worry about is New Year's Eve. I haven't slept well for the past three nights. I guess I'm all keyed up.

Wednesday, December 20, 1939

I got a gorgeous strapless formal at *The Sample Shop*. It's crushed strawberry color with a velvet bodice. Do I look like a dream in it!

I went to have cocktails at the Park Club tonight with Nan. I'm so happy for her. She has a date for New Year's Eve. She met this boy Robert when bowling one night, and they just hit it off. Wouldn't it be wonderful if he could see past the scars and see how perfect she truly is?

Wonder of wonders Don bumped into me at the bar and said he had been planning to stop over later and ask me out for New Year's Eve. Everything is lining up perfectly. I hope that is an indication of what the coming year is going to bring.

Friday, December 22, 1939

I thought 5 o'clock would never come. I'm so excited. No work all day tomorrow. Life is too wonderful. Don was over tonight. He, Dad, Mother and I played a great game of bridge. The older generation only licked us by 170 points. We had scotch and rye adding to the holiday cheer. I can't get over the change in Don. He's not bashful at all anymore about kissing me. He doesn't tease me anymore. Wow! I'm completely surprised.

We decided to take a long walk in the snow. It was perfect for this time of year. Big white flakes were falling so slowly from the sky; just like in the movies. We talked about family and the future of our country. We talked about what it's like to be young during this time. There was a rim of snow on the scarf around his neck, and I dusted it off and kissed him. Winter can be fun. He stayed until 2:30 a.m.

Sunday, December 24, 1939 Christmas Eve

Today was perfect! We had a lot of company and a lot of drinks. Don, Nan, Margaret, Bee, Bud, the boss and his wife and of course, Uncle George, Aunt Milly and the girls were all celebrating with us. I drank all afternoon – rye, beer, wine and scotch.

We all crowded around the piano and sang *Jingle Bells, Joy to the World* and a great rendition of *The Twelve Days of Christmas*. This year I got to sing "Five Golden Rings."

Don cooked supper here, and I set the table and made soup. We also did the dishes. Mistletoe was in action. Don did all right. He and I went to church and then to Coles. We came home and sat on the davenport and looked at our beautiful tree. It looks gorgeous. I hate to have this night end.

Monday, December 25, 1939

It was another perfect Christmas again. I got gorgeous lingerie, perfume, a chenille robe, cosmetics and a lovely necklace and earring set, red stones. Don gave me a bottle of *Lentheric Anticipation* perfume.

Mitch and Chuck dropped in this evening as well. We had a swell turkey dinner and our table looked beautiful as it does every year. I look forward to the time when I will set the table for my husband, children, family and friends. Mother and Dad will be so proud.

Then I went to the college ball with Tommy. I had on my new evening dress from *The Sample Shop* and my squirrel jacket. I had a perfect time. We had so much fun, dancing and laughing. I felt like the belle of the ball. What a wonderful time of life this is. I got in at 5:30 a.m.

Sunday, December 31, 1939

Ending up this year I haven't had a moment to write in my diary. I've had some catching up to do with the books at work. I'm so relieved that everything struck perfectly. Not a penny off.

I was awfully nervous all day about tonight. I worry so, it makes me mad. Don sent me a green orchid which just about floored me. I looked perfect tonight. The orchid looked gorgeous on my pink off the shoulder dress. Don thought I looked super. He wore a tux and looked so dashing. We went to the Peter Stuyvesant room and boy was it crowded! It cost $6.00 a couple just for a reservation. Our drinks for a dozen people came to $16.75 which wasn't so bad. Don had a flask in his pocket and nipped at it all through the night.

When the clock struck midnight confetti rained down an

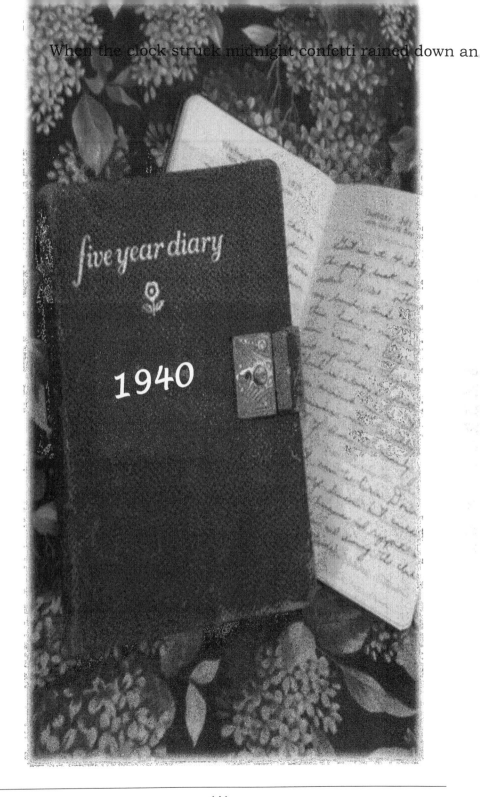

Monday, January 1, 1940

We visited the Statler for cocktails after midnight. What a whirlwind of an evening. Don got me home at 5:35 a.m. I had a nice farewell kiss. It didn't totally make up for being left at midnight, but he explained that he was outside with the guys. He is leaving this afternoon at 1:00 p.m., and he wanted to have a little time with his friends. I have no idea how he can do it. He drank nonstop all evening. I slept in until 1:00 p.m.

    I feel very low tonight. The bottom seems to have dropped out of everything. I pray that 1940 will be as good to me as 1939. I looked up the words to the New Year's Eve song that everyone always sings at midnight. I can't say that I completely understand the lyrics, but friendship and kindness ring through it, and sadness too.

Auld Lang Syne

Should auld acquaintance be forgot
And never brought to mind
Should auld acquaintance be forgot
And days of auld lang syne
And there's a hand, my trusty friend
And gie's a hand to thine
We'll take a cup of kindness yet
For auld lang syne

For auld lang syne, my dear
For auld lang syne
We'll take a cup of kindness yet
For auld lang syne

Should auld acquaintance be forgot
And never brought to mind
Should auld acquaintance be forgot
And days of auld lang syne

For auld lang syne, my dear
For auld lang syne
Should auld acquaintance be forgot
And days of auld lang syne
For auld lang syne

Friday, January 5, 1940

I worked like a Trojan all day. We are moving the office on Wednesday. I have to write Don tonight. Gee! I miss him so.

Bee and Nan came over and we played bridge with Mother. I'm so lucky to have a Mother who can relate to my friends. She's like one of the gang. Dad is at a stag party tonight. I'm sure he'll behave. After all, it is Dad.

Saturday, January 6, 1940

I had cramps all day today, but nevertheless I went to see *Hunchback of Notre Dame* with Bee. It was perfect. So sad, and that new actress, Maureen O'Hara, was simply darling.

I made reservations for the premiere of *Gone With The Wind*. I can hardly wait!

Surprise of the day; Mother bought a Persian lamb coat at Ullman's. It will be out Tuesday. Mother is such a beautiful dresser. She has such style and grace. What a wonderful example she sets for me.

They played the most romantic songs on the radio tonight. Never have I missed Don as much as these days. Is it really love? I wonder.

Sunday, January 7, 1940

I wrote to Don. After I posted the letter I realized that I forgot to tell him he has my cigarette case. Souvenir?

I saw John tonight at our youth group. He looked perfect. He played the piano beautifully in the reception room. It was empty with the exception of the two of us. He played a lovely sonata just for me. In the face of such an attractive young man I never forgot Don. I keep wondering what he's doing all of the time. I hope to Heaven he settles down to good hard work minus the liquor. He has a brilliant future ahead of him if he lives right.

Chuck was over while I was gone. The old love is on the scene more and more.

Friday, January 12, 1940

The boss left for Florida this morning. I went downtown on the Williamsville bus, which I catch across the street. I picked up my tickets for *Gone With the Wind*. The first night is all sold out. I bought a Literary Guild book, *No Arms, No Armor*.

Mother washed my hair before she and Dad went out. I stayed in and finished Vera Britain's "*Honorable Estate*." I don't know when I've read a book that has affected me so profoundly. It was truly magnificent!

Sunday, January 14, 1940

I started *A Half Inch of Candle*. It is marvelous and just my type of story. Bee was over this afternoon. We talked about boys and life and love. Then we headed off to rehearsal. They still haven't gotten to my part yet. John is grand in his part. He really should pursue a career on the stage.

We went over to Bee's house afterwards, and John played the piano. *Sibelius Valse Triste* he plays so beautifully. I shut my eyes and I am swept away, and my heart is lifted so high.

John is darling, so handsome, but still such a cynic. I don't see how anyone could fail to be happy in this age.

Monday, January 15, 1940

Everything is dull, no real business coming in. Bud says that is to be expected in January. No one buys anything in January. Of course I still have loads of fun at work, and I get to read when nothing else is expected of me. There was a high wind blowing all day. With the woods across the street as yet undeveloped, the landscape looked very desolate, like *Wuthering Heights*.

Bud took me to lunch. It was so kind of him. We had a sandwich at The Wishing Well Restaurant. We even had a beer to go with it. I don't really consider that drinking in the afternoon. After all, it wasn't a sidecar or anything.

I wrote a letter to Don. Bee called up and wanted to meet me downtown after work to see a movie. We saw Bette Davis and Errol Flynn in *Private Lives of Elizabeth of Essex*. It held me spellbound! What an actress she is! And what a specimen of a man he is. Oh! When she slapped him with such a crack across his beautiful face I felt it in my heart. I have never slapped a man across the face. I've never had a need to. I can't imagine ever having to do something like that. I know I could never slap Errol Flynn across the face no matter what he said or did.

Thursday, January 18, 1940

I drove Bud's Plymouth to lunch today. He's awfully nice about letting me borrow it. It's still pretty slow at work so I've been reading *Jamaica Inn* practically all day. What a wonderful read.

Very stormy tonight. I walked to Nan's for bridge club. I had a swell time although Martha and I held bum cards all evening.

I came home to find Chuck talking with the family. A year ago my heart would have beat fast at the sight of him. Time changes things.

Saturday, January 20, 1940

I didn't have to work this morning. I was cleaning the silver when Carol called up and said the house was on fire. I rushed over to their house. The hot water tank had exploded. It was in the front page of the evening paper.

The storm kept up with such strength. It's terrific – plenty cold too! Dad won $30 at poker this afternoon. What luck!

I read and studied my part in the play tonight. I finished *Jamaica Inn*. It was just as thrilling as the movie. I've just started *Wind, Sand & Stars*.

Thursday, January 25, 1940

At last! The long waited night. I dressed up in my new outfit. I want to feel the part of going to an actual premier.

It's such a story night – however nothing daunted us. We had dinner at the Peter Stuyvesant Room, perfection in itself.

Mere words can never describe the thrill of seeing the title *Gone With The Wind* sweep across the screen. My heart was beating right out of my chest. I was not alone. I could see how everyone in the theater was beyond themselves with excitement. It is more than a movie – it is a milestone. Generations from now people will still be talking about this beautiful film and the beautiful people in it. The Technicolor is gorgeous. The acting of Vivien Leigh and Clark Gable and the whole cast is beyond reproach. Nothing can or ever will equal this motion picture.

Saturday, January 27, 1940

I saw *Gone With The Wind* for the second time with Carol and Laura. I was just as excited and thrilled as before. But it leaves you with a feeling that your own life is very inconsequential. I can't get that picture out of my head. I bought the movie edition of the book and even some Scarlett cologne. What a sap I am.

I don't see how the movie got past the censors. It followed the book perfectly. Rhett and Scarlett's love scenes would take the breath out of you. Everything pales into insignificance because the three hours and forty minutes of drama, love, thrills and comedy. I'll never forget it!

It all makes me so mad. Why can't my life be exciting like *Gone With The Wind*? Something must happen to make my life new.

Friday, February 2, 1940

There was a small error in the books, and Bud and I worked on it for several hours until I found it. Bud was exceptionally swell today. Incidentally he wants to take me to the Chef's Café some night. Hmmm. Wonder what his wife would think of that?

Ruth, Nan and I went to a fortune teller down in the Italian section. She told me I was going to fall in love soon and marry. She said I naturally attracted money and that I would never have to worry about financial matters as long as I live. I only wish I could count on what she foretold.

Saturday, February 3, 1940

I cleaned my room completely and ironed some hankies and napkins. I read and lay around the rest of the day. I was alone in the house tonight; I had plenty of time for meditation. I know now what causes my restless feelings. I'm waiting for the one to come along. I do hope that happens soon.

Tuesday, February 6, 1940

I had a riot at the office. It's more like a party than work. Bud makes me so mad at times, but I like him in spite of it.

Chuck came over tonight. I was quite surprised. We all played Chinese checkers. Chuck's mother is in bed with coronary thrombosis. He is very worried about her. I think that's why he came over here. He feels this is like home to him. We are always so happy and enjoying ourselves. He is still as darling as ever but the flame isn't there anymore.

Saturday, February 10, 1940

I went downtown with Carol. I paid $15 on my fur jacket which brings the balance down to $45. I also bought a striped tailored blouse, two pairs of my favorite shade stocking – "Wine Glow" and a rhinestone bracelet. I still have $40 left in the bank but there probably won't be much left of that after I have my wisdom teeth pulled.

Nan came over and we played Chinese checkers and bridge. *Gone With The Wind* is in its 3rd week downtown. I can't see them ever pulling it.

Wednesday, February 14, 1940

There was a swell storm in progress when I woke up this morning. It is desolate out at the office.

John called and asked me to go bowling with him. Voelker's Bowling Lanes has been around forever. We ran into Nan and Robert. What a nice guy he is, and he really seems to like Nan quite a bit. John loves bowling; he seems to enjoy himself. A rather lowbrow crowd, but I always have a good time.

Friday, February 16, 1940

Our roof caught on fire about 7:15 tonight! Mother and Dad had just left for the movies. Some man rang the doorbell and told me. The engine got here, and the firemen dragged the hose all the way up the stairs to the attic. It was a panic. The fire didn't amount to much, thank God! Chuck came over and took me out to get something to eat and a couple of beers. I have to be careful with beer; it's so filling and not at all good for the figure.

Thursday, February 29, 1940

I certainly was rushed all day. Boy! It feels good to be really working again. The boss anticipated a big year. I'm getting several new responsibilities at work. I'm turning into quite the career woman, that's me!

Who knows, maybe that is the road for me: career, travel? Who am I kidding? I want love and security in my life.

Friday, March 1, 1940

I was busy all day. It seemed like old times and I was darn glad. It will be like this from April 1st on.

I was reading *Gone With The Wind* tonight when who should come over but Chuck. He has been over three times when we weren't home. We went out to Coles and then parked after that. He has changed a great deal – he's more subdued, dignified and no more smart aleck stuff. I am glad. I guess he still has that "old feeling" about me. I'll have to admit that it's ditto for me too.

Sunday, March 3, 1940

Vivien Leigh got the Academy Award for the year's best acting in *Gone With The Wind*. It cleaned up on eight other awards too.

John called and picked me up to go bowling again. I bowled four games and my best score was the last one – 92. I like it so much I wish I could really get good. Perhaps I misjudged this game.

Wednesday, March 6, 1940

Boy am I tired! I had a swell time at work. Bud and I are getting along swell although he teases me something terrible.

Mother has changed my room around. It looks simply divine; if it would only stay that way. I played bridge again with Mother, Dad and Bee. It was a nice quiet evening then Carol and Laura came over and we all went to the movies to see *A Child is Born*. Was it sad! It was all about motherhood, and it just about broke my heart in two. It begged the question, what kind of mother will I be? I have such a grand example to follow.

Mother, Bee and I settled in after we dropped the girls off. Mother made a nice pot of tea for us, and we had a grand gab session. We talked about sex, and Mother answered a lot of our questions. They were rather tame questions, but she did a good job.

Friday, March 15, 1940

Still having a hilarious time at the office. How can this be called work? I told Mother and Dad that I wouldn't exchange my job for that of J.P. Morgan's secretary. I truly feel like an adult. That sense of independence is building up inside of me.

I went to the Touraine Lounge with Tommy who is in town. We had a grand time my old friend and me. It was odd how quiet it was there on a Friday evening. We had the entire place to ourselves for a good part of the night. I had a Sherry Flip and three-year old scotch. We talked about everything from philosophy to sex, to how to smoke gracefully. He's such a wonderful friend. It's nice to have a fellow for a friend, a real friend. I don't ever have to worry about Tommy making a move. I got in just before midnight.

Tuesday, March 19, 1940

All day I have been thinking about the records I was listening to last night. *Romeo & Juliet Fantasy*, Tchaikovsky's violin concerto and the overture to *Tannhauser*, all perfectly marvelous. I'm set on the idea of buying a record player and collecting records. The boss sent me downtown to pick up some plans and blueprints. While I was waiting for them to get done I went across the street to Denton, Cottier and Daniels. I priced a Stromberg Carlson record player – a lovely walnut one at $24.95. I'd love to have it. It will be an investment I know I'll never regret. I'll save up for it and buy all Tchaikovsky records. Music is something that is truly healing and comforting. I remember when Dada was quietly making her way to the other side; we had borrowed a record player and played her favorite music. She was lulled to heaven by Brahms and Mozart. I can think of no better way to pass over.

Sunday, March 24, 1940 – Easter Sunday

It was a lovely cold day, plenty of sun but very cool temperatures. I wore my squirrel jacket and new hat to church. The service was beautiful. The sun shining through the stained glass is so inspiring, such rich and vibrant colors. I closed my eyes and prayed to God that our country, our world would stay safe from hateful, powerful and destructive forces, forces with bald heads and silly mustaches.

I gave Mother a dozen roses for Easter, yellow roses. We had a ham dinner, and Mother did a grand job of it. The apple muffins I made were a great hit. Mother had a basket for me, how sweet of her to always make each holiday magical and loving. Easter is such a wonderful holiday. You simply know that spring and warm weather are just around the corner.

Monday, March 25, 1940

It is thawing a little. How all this now will ever melt, I don't know. I had a swell time at the office as usual. I got the curse this morning – cramps weren't as bad.

I went to the movies with Bee and Nan. It was swell; James Stewart and Margaret Sullivan in *Shop around the Corner*. Jimmy Stewart is the perfect example of the shy type of lover, and sometimes I think I'd like to marry that sort of a man. They're quite fascinating in a way all their own.

Friday, March 29, 1940

Bud had big news today. His wife is going to have a baby. It's quite far off. I blushed fifteen colors when he told me.

I went over to Margaret's for dinner tonight. Her parents were out for the evening. I had such a big appetite. Margaret makes the most divine pies. She should open up a shop. So few people can make crust the way she does, so tender and flaky.

We had a long confidential talk during the evening, quite long in fact. As usual we got on our pet subject, sex, It made me think of my old flame, Chuck. He never seems to stray very far from my thoughts when I am talking about my pet subject.

I bought some new nail polish today. It has a dark pink hue to it.

Saturday, March 30, 1940

How very strange. Chuck and Mitch came over tonight. Chuck and I went on the side porch alone and had a long talk. God! I am going crazy right this minute. He said I'd never be able to erase the memory of his love making no matter who I married. He went on to say a lot of wonderful and terrible things at the same time. As I write this I am afraid – afraid that what he said will be the truth.

Monday, April 1, 1940

I've been thinking over all the stuff that Chuck said

the other night and I'm convinced most of it was a line. I'm not in love with him so why should I worry about it? The day when I meet a man whose character is as nice as his love making, then I'll fall. Character and integrity are the utmost important characteristic in a good man. And that's what I'm looking for, a good man.

John stopped over tonight. We had a very intellectual evening drinking beer and talking about poetry and philosophy.

Thursday, April 4, 1940

I got a letter from Don! I guess miracles do happen. He didn't come home because his vacation was too short. He said he and Mary Ruth definitely broke up, as if I didn't know they would. I'm so pleased that he wrote to me though. Maybe he's clearing the decks for this summer.

Bee and I had dinner at Laube's Old Spain then we went to see Errol Flynn in *Virginia City* which was truly super colossal terrific. Errol drove me nuts as usual. Too bad he's the only man alive like him. I got so excited during the picture that my hands perspired and the black came off my gloves onto my hands. Sort of silly maybe but I couldn't help it. My body just reacts to him.

Sunday, April 7, 1940

It felt perfect to be able to sleep in. I luxuriated and how! I do deserve it. I have been working very hard.

I made this a "Deborah" day. I read and listened to the radio until 10 o'clock. In my moments of solitude, I dreamed dreams that no one knows of but myself, dreams of a new life under new skies, with new opportunities. Someday I'm going to have a boat and go sailing and feel the water running over the deck.

I wonder, I've been writing in my diaries for eight years now. Writing down very personal thoughts about who I am and what I want out of life. Will someone read this someday? Will my daughter read this? What a thought!

Tuesday, April 9, 1940

The war in Europe has taken a sudden new turn. This morning Germany invaded Denmark and now they are capturing cities in Norway. It is all so terrible. Now, it is indeed a world conflict.

Bud sold two houses today. The boss is flying to New York tonight to the F.H.A. office. He is tickled pink at the way things are going in the housing market.

Chuck was over tonight. His love making is divine as usual. However, I only care for him in that one way. I do so hope that my husband someday has the same skills that Chuck has. It is a skill every married man should have.

Chuck is so damn pro-German it makes my blood boil.

Wednesday, April 10, 1940

I wrote to Don today. I put in a few cutting remarks – not bad but with a little edge on them.

The war is raging all over the place. The British are landing troops in Norway and Sweden. They've got to get the Germans out of there so they can't bomb England. What a mess!

Sunday, April 14, 1940

I caught up on a lot of sleep, even took a nap in the afternoon. I do so love doing that.

The war news is hot! All the commentators seem to think that Hitler has bitten off more than he can chew. I hope to God he has.

I read *Kitty Foyle* for a whil e. It is truly a fine social study of the white collar girl. It has a lot of pathos in spite of the humor in the way Kitty talks. She's so in love, and love can make a girl do crazy things, or at least take steps that are not well thought out. I'll have to remember that.

I went to bed early tonight. My pillows are so plush and cozy.

Thursday, April 18, 1940

Everybody wished me a happy birthday first thing this morning. It doesn't seem possible that I'm twenty. In that length of time again I'll be forty, then sixty. I hate to think of that though.

Bee gave me a swell surprise party and I was nearly knocked over; Norma, Nan, Martha, Ruth and Margaret were there. They all gave me lovely presents. Bee gave me *Intermezzo* and *Night & Day* records. Of course Mother and Dad gave me *Romeo & Juliet Fantasy*. It was a perfect evening. Mrs. Brown and Betty came over to wish me many happy returns of the day, and I got a dozen of Mrs. Brown's famous chocolate chip cookies.

Sunday, April 21, 1940

I slept in as usual. How I love Sunday! The kids came over and we played the record player most of the day. We have the windows open and you can smell spring all around us as well as Sunday dinners cooking. I love to have the windows open.

Uncle George, Laura, Carol and Aunt Helen came over for dinner. Aunt Milly wasn't feeling well. We are quite a bunch of characters. Our family is really the wackiest bunch I've ever heard of. We laughed most of the evening.

Tuesday, April 23, 1940

I feel lousy and tired. I have some life decisions to make. I'm very nervous about what I'm going to do with my life. Truly, what am I going to do? I just don't know. I cannot think about it anymore tonight. I am going to go to bed at 8 o'clock, which is right now. I'm going to read and lose my mind in what the characters are dong and not think of anything else. Thank God for books! What would I do without them!

Sunday, April 28, 1940

I'm so pleased that Mother and Dad took a trip. They so deserve it. I think it's grand that Dad bought tickets to the Broadway show *Old Acquaintance*. Mother will simply love it!

I'm also thrilled that Bee stayed the night last night. We lingered over breakfast. I washed dishes and she dried. I vacuumed and cleaned the living room and dining room. I dusted bedroom floors. Bee took care of the fireplace ashes. We stayed up quite late in front of the fire talking. Wouldn't it be fun to have an apartment together; but not in Buffalo. I've got to start thinking about where I want to live.

Friday, May 10, 1940

Startling but not surprising events in Europe today: Germany has invaded the Netherlands, Belgium and a part of France. Hitler is really going to town. It seems that the U.S. entering the war is imminent now. I am so fearful for all of the young men I know. I want them all to be safe.

Wednesday, May 22, 1940

There was plenty of war news today. Britain is now a dictatorship in order to meet the emergency of threatened invasion by Germany. Winston Churchill and his government have the power to conscript men and wealth. All munitions factories are working 24 hours a day seven days a week.

Meanwhile the French have recaptured Arras and Abbeville, two very strategic positions.

The war is raging. The Germans are only 22 miles from Dover. The allied armies are trying to cut through the German wedge so as to release the arms caught in a trap.

Bridge Club tonight, we talked war more than we played bridge. I am getting to be a regular fanatic on the subject, and for good reason.

Friday, May 24, 1940

It rained all last night. I had both windows wide open to listen to it.

I got another letter from Don. He'll be home a week from Saturday.

King George spoke today. In simple words he described the terrible impending danger England is in. All we can do is pray. Oh, how very different our lives are now.

Sunday, May 26, 1940

I had cramps all day. I was so disappointed because I wanted to enjoy the new Buick Dad brought home yesterday. It was such a lovely day too. However, I pushed myself and got up to go for a ride. We went out to the office and looked at some of the houses. It is so funny and strange to think of all the young couples who will be living and loving and building families in these homes. I don't know: am I envious or running for the hills?

I came home and went to bed before eight. I listened to some news flashes. The Germans say they are going to use some new horrible weapon in their invasion of the British Isles. It is so terrible to feel so powerless in the face of all of this turmoil. We must all unite against this horrific turn of events.

Tuesday, May 28, 1940

This morning King Leopold of Belgium surrendered to Germany. He is being bitterly criticized and rightly so. Now there is a huge gap in the allied lines because of the withdrawal of Belgian troops. The allies are fighting valiantly in spite of this disaster.

Ruth and I went to see *Lights Out in Europe* telling the story in actual pictures of Europe before the second Great War and after France and England had declared war on Germany. It was a very graphic documentary of the world's worst catastrophe.

Thursday, May 30, 1940 Memorial Day

Today bombs are raining on France. Flanders is the scene of the most terrible fighting that the world has ever seen.

We went with the Marvins to Chestnut Ridge Park. We had a grand time. We rode in the Boston Hills in Dad's new Buick. The countryside was beautiful, lush and green. It reminded me of the fields of France. Our country is so beautiful; I hope no destruction ever reaps a harvest here. This is still the land of the free and the home of the brave.

I wonder if I should join up and help serve our country? I'll have to give this some real thought.

Friday, May 31, 1940

I had my hair set tonight. Also had an oil shampoo which makes a great improvement in my hair.

The British are evacuating Flanders, covered by a rear guard of French troops. One British captain, back in England, spoke on the radio tonight. He said "The British have lost many battles, but never the last." Let us hope it comes true in this war.

Vivien Leigh and Laurence Olivier have been called back to England for war service.

Saturday, June 1, 1940

I couldn't go downtown because it rained so hard. It was fate working I guess, because Don came over this afternoon. He got in last night at eleven. He doesn't look very good. He has a cold and looks tired. I certainly hope he has curtailed his heavy drinking. That can do terrible things to your body if you overindulge. He was driving his father's Cadillac coupe.

I didn't think I'd be having a date al all tonight but Don invited me over to his house to play bridge with his parents. I had a lovely time even though I had terrible cards. Their home is very nice, just what you'd imagine.

Sunday, June 2, 1940

Beautiful day but it is all lost by war. The B.E.F. in Flanders has accomplished what is hailed as a military miracle. Four-fifths of the B.E.F has been evacuated from the Flanders death trap back to England. It is very heartening to the morale of the allies. We all feel that right will triumph in the end and the allies will be victorious. Hitler's plan for world domination must never be put into effect.

I prayed and prayed today that peace will come to the world.

Tuesday, June 4, 1940

The weather is starting to get hot. It is a blessed relief from our horrid spring.

The war situation was sort of quiet. Paris was bombed yesterday, but the damage was not very severe and the same with loss of life. Italy has not yet entered the war. If Mussolini would only use his brains and stay out of it. Winston Churchill made a stirring speech to the House of Commons today expressing his thoughts: "We shall never surrender!"

Friday, June 7, 1940

Our first really hot day. I could have gotten a swell tan if I could sun myself in the back yard of the office. Don't think that would go over very well.

According to reports, the war is going satisfactorily for the French. Our country is prepared to send every conceivable aid except manpower to the allies. I think it is absolutely the only thing to do.

Wonder of all: Chuck came over. I thought he wouldn't after the way I treated him.
I was polite, but he was a mighty poor substitute for Don. Why hasn't Don called or stopped by?

Monday, June 10, 1940

Italy has declared war on France and England. Now it all looks so terrible.

Don came over! He has been in all weekend with a cold. I do wish he had called me. At least we could have talked on the phone. He needn't have worried then about passing his cold on to me. I wouldn't have cared.

We listened to a speech by President Roosevelt at a graduation in Charlotte, N.C. It was a powerful denunciation of Mussolini and also it told, in no uncertain terms, where we stand in this world of chaos.

Don stayed and we played bridge with Mother and Dad. He was very quiet. I'm certain that he was thinking about what role he might play in this war. I was thinking the very same thing.

Wednesday, June 12, 1940

I got up feeling fit as a fiddle. I'm getting into this routine of late nights. I'm more than satisfied with Don. He is simply adorable. When I'm not with him I keep getting the emptiest nervous feeling in my stomach. It's awful.

Our bridge club went out to The Quaker Bonnet in Orchard Park to eat. I took the Buick and passed the 500 – mile mark. I let it out. Boy! Does it ride like wings. I had a marvelous dinner. I ate way too much.

Thursday, June 13, 1940

The Germans are all around Paris, and it looks mighty bad. The French are not going to fight in Paris because they want to save the city. Premier Reynaud declared they will keep on fighting until the last man has fallen.

Bee and I went to the U.B. play at the Studio Theater with Tommy and his cousin. The play was *Night Must Fall.* What a terrifying play. It simply gives you chills. I did love the movie with Robert Montgomery and Rosalind Russell. That is one of my favorite mystery movies.

Friday, June 14, 1940

Paris is now in German hands. The Nazis and their war machine rolled down the Champs-Elysees. To think that we, in this generation, could witness such a thing! My heart is too heavy for words. What are we to do? The French are still fighting; they will never give in.

Don called me up from Cherry Hill about dinnertime. We're going to the Cherry Hill dance tomorrow night. He also asked for a date tonight but I went to the movies with Nan and Margaret. I can't be called up and expected to go out on a date with such little notice. He must learn.

Oh how beautiful the lilacs smell! Mother brought a bouquet of them into my room and placed them in a crystal vase my bed. I listened to the radio and tried not to get a news station. I wanted to listen to beautiful romantic music to lift me up out of the sadness that the world is experiencing. Paris needs our prayers tonight. Tonight I will pray on my knees.

Sunday, June 16, 1940

I got in at 4:00 a.m. this morning. I got up early to help Carol with her French. I had a wonderful time last night. Don looked like Robert Taylor in his dinner jacket. How devastating he looked. I couldn't help but envision what he would or will look like in uniform.

Don picked me up around noon to go on a picnic. Thank goodness Mother inquired as to what he had prepared to eat. He had two bottles of soda and one peanut butter sandwich, rather unappetizing to say the least. Of course Mother pulled out our picnic hamper and filled it with cold chicken, homemade sweet rolls, two beers, some carrot sticks and two pieces of strawberry pie!

We went for a long ride and went to Olcott Beach for the day. We stopped for some Bye's Popcorn, a darling little popcorn stand a family has by the road in Newfane. Don was very appreciative of Mother's efforts; so was I.

What a beautiful moon tonight. There was a bonfire on the beach, and we were invited to join a bunch of kids who were crowded around it. Don had a blanket in his car, and he wrapped us up in it. He didn't do too badly by the campfire tonight. He is damn puzzling when it comes to love making.

I listened to the news on the way home. The present French cabinet has collapsed and Premier Paul Reynaud, who advocated a fight to the finish, resigned. Marshal Petain is now premier.

Monday, June 17, 1940

France surrendered this morning. One can hardly blame them because Germany is in complete control of the military resources. Now Great Britain is alone fighting Germany and Italy. There now certainly is no doubt that the world is being encircled by Nazis. We are in terrible danger, and that is putting it mildly. There is a certainty I think that the U.S. will be in the war. It seems incredible that I am living in the most terrible era history has ever known. God help us keep our freedom.

Tuesday, June 18, 1940

Everything is war! I heard a re-broadcast of Churchill's speech. It was so noble and sublime. Surely God in his Heaven cannot let him down. If Britain loses, the world is in for another dark age.

Washington is burning the midnight oil in speeding up preparedness. Every minute, every hour of the day I pray for the French and British and my own dear country.

I talked with Don for quite a long time on the phone. He seemed so interested in everything I had to say. It was a lovely conversation. I wish we could have more of them. I can never count on him to be the same from day to day.

Wednesday, June 19, 1940

We went to Laura's graduation at #81. She was easily the loveliest child there. Six years ago I graduated, but it seems like a lifetime ago. We are all so proud of her. She's always been a very bright girl. She graduated top of her class.

Don got a 77 at Cherry Hill today playing golf. He is very proud of it and more than a little conceited. We played bridge tonight and lost to Mother and Dad. Don gave me a huge talk on the war which really is quite sensible. I guess he thinks I'm quite hysterical and amusing. He makes me furious sometimes.

Sunday, June 23, 1940

Perfectly terrible day. It rained from the afternoon on. We spent the day at Chamber's beach house. I had been planning on working on my tan. We played bridge all day into the evening. Thank goodness Ruth is here. We took a break and sat out on the screened-in porch. I love the sound that the rain made tapping on the roof. It all smelled so earthy and wonderful. I asked Ruth what she thought about all of this terrible war news. I asked her if she was afraid. She said she tried not to think about it. How can we not think about it?

I have given a lot of my clothes to Les de la France. They have a war relief bureau on Parker near Hertel. They are collecting whatever people can send to help the people of France. We cannot put a blind eye to what is going on in the world.

Wednesday, June 26, 1940

I sure am getting used to this late night stuff. I feel dead in the morning but after I eat lunch I feel tip-top again.

Things are pretty quiet in Europe which means that Hitler is probably preparing for the worst campaign his fiendish mind can invent for the British. Today he visited Napoleon's Tomb and the Eiffel Tower in Paris. It's almost a sacrilege to think of him walking over such ground. There really isn't much we can do right now but pray.

Thursday, June 27, 1940

The Republican National Convention is in full swing. Their platform slogan is "Peace, preparedness, prosperity." It's nice work if you can get it. I hope Wendell Willkie gets the nomination, and I wouldn't mind seeing him president.

Practiced on my golf at Erin Down and then played four holes with Dad. I have improved immensely over last year, which encourages me a great deal. I had several good shots. I hope I do as well at Cherry Hill on Sunday.

Friday, June 28, 1940

Wendell Willkie got the nomination. I guess the crowded at the convention went wild. I do hope he becomes president but it depends on the foreign situation.

Russia has moved into Romania, and I think it has the Germans a little worried. The Germans aren't the only ones who are worried. Mother and Dad assure me that everything is going to be all right.

Don came over and we played bridge. While he was here John called. It's funny how he calls up out of the blue. He wanted to know if I'd like to take a ride. I told him that I had company but another time for certain.

Don took me to Coles after we played several games with Mother and Dad. We sat in a booth in the bar, and I tried to explain my fears about the war. I asked him if he was thinking about what his role might be. He looked at me with a rather queer expression, as though he hadn't given it any thought at all. It appears that I had been misreading him.

Wednesday, July 3, 1940

Don came over tonight. He was in a wonderful mood. Nan was here too. We played bridge after Dad got home from the club.

Don gave me a couple of good spankings. It was fun and I enjoyed it but he doesn't know that. He is still the world's biggest enigma and he revels in it.

All this time, my life is moving peacefully on but the scene in Europe is ever rapidly shifting. The expected blitzing on England is awaited any day now. I truly wish there was more that I could do. I don't want to passively sit by and watch the world implode. I want to take some sort of action.

Sunday, July 7, 1940

I slept until about twelve thirty. It was luxurious. I slept some more in the afternoon until Ruth came over and asked me to go to the New Park Zoo with her.

Don didn't feel so hot last night so I imagine he's taking it easy today. (I hope.)

I tried to catch up on my correspondence. I feel terrible that I haven't written to Aunt Helen in weeks.

The British are really taking the bull by the horns. They've recaptured a lot of French battleships, and Hitler is plenty mad about it all.

How can Hitler have so much power? He looks like a man with no power behind him. Why are so many people in Germany listening to him?

Tuesday, July 8, 1940

This has been the first really hot day in a long time. It is very cool in the office though, so it's hard to tell what it's like outside. I have been looking longingly out the window at the kids playing in the street. Sometimes I wish I were a kid again.

In tonight's editorial Dorothy Thompson predicts a dire future for the U.S. It really makes you feel terrible! Some might call her an alarmist, but then again she may have real foresight.

I played nine holes of golf with Dad. I had a lot of good shots and feel that I'm really improving with each game I play. It's grand having this time with Dad. And he could be playing with his friends. We went for a cocktail afterwards. I'm so glad I was able to get out of work early to spend some time with him. Mother and I have so much quality time together.

I had a cocktail with Mother when I got home. Just one and then off to bed after dinner, a beautiful day with two of my favorite people.

Thursday, July 11, 1940

The weather is still very cool, so strange for July. I can't remember a summer being so autumnal. I could use a nice hot day. Bee, Mother and I went to the movies today downtown; we saw Olivia deHavilland and Jeffrey Lynn in *My Love Come Back*. It was very entertaining. The music in it was heavenly.

I really need a new bathing suit. I have outgrown my old one in just the right places. I'm sure Mother will take me downtown to buy one. Maybe I can get a matching cover up jacket as well.

Monday, July 15, 1940

The Germans and Italians are certainly taking a long time before their invasion of England. Churchill says the English will see London in ruins before allowing them to be victorious. It all sounds swell but I only hope he means it.

Thursday, July 18, 1940

I saw the most marvelous story today. Merle Oberon and the devastating George Brent in *Til We Meet Again*. It was very beautiful and so sad. Gee! It makes you so dissatisfied with life. I wish something wonderful would happen to me, some wonderful forbidden man just like Brent's character in the movie. Of course I wouldn't want him to be a felon.

I wonder when he'll come along, if he even does exist. Somehow I feel that Don and everyone else I've known are just "flashes in the pan," so to speak.

Saturday, July 20, 1940

Don picked me up and did he look smooth. He does have a smile about him. He took me to a cute roadhouse he discovered the other night called "The Wishing Well." It actually has an authentic one outside that's 125years old. The bar is down in their cellar, how clandestine. I guess not many people know about it.

The war news is better and better. Hitler has made a speech, giving Britain a last chance to make peace (on German terms of course) before he destroys the Empire. The British are cold to his proposal, and I don't blame them. That propaganda worked with other European countries, but not with the British!

Monday, July 22, 1940

It's a terrifically hot day; I took a bath as soon as I got home. How cool and soothing the water felt.

Dad, Mother, Don and I played bridge. Mother was fanning herself with a beautiful fan Aunt Milly gave her. It's so lovely and delicate, but it does the trick.

Chuck came over out of the blue. He ruined a perfectly good evening. I suppose he and Don went out beering afterward. It makes me so darn mad. I don't get it. Chuck socked him last summer. You would think that Don would stay away from a character like that, but no it's just the opposite. And then there's Chuck. He's made it quite clear to me in the past that he doesn't like or trust Don. Men are a total mystery to me.

I love my new bathing suit, white with red roses.

Thursday, July 25, 1940

Dad left for Detroit this morning. I miss Dad when he's gone. Even though he's not a big talker the house seems quieter when he's not here.

Don came over tonight. We took another ride. We stopped at the Military Grill and the Wishing Well. I got gloriously tight on only five glasses of beer. We drove a long way after that. Don was never sweeter. He says I'm more congenial when I'm tight. I say the same for him.

Saturday, July 27, 1940

It rained today – a blessed relief from the heat. I took a nap for a few hours. The soft rain tapping on the roof lulled me to sleep. For some reason I always sleep so soundly when it's raining out. And I have the most wonderful dreams.

Margaret came over and Mother peeked her head in my room to see if I wanted to come down. Of course I did. Mother, Margaret and I sat on the side porch. We had a long gab fest about everything under the sun, or should I say under the rain? Mother told us that there is some special someone out there for each of us.

Since we were in such a lovely and open minded setting I decided to ask Mother a rather delicate question about marriage. I asked her about the physical side of marriage. Of course Margaret and I know the mechanics of it all, but how often is considered normal in a healthy marriage.

Mother looked at me and took a deep breath and explained her take on the subject. "Deborah, you are 20 years old and old enough, I feel, to know the honest truth. And I'm sure Margaret that you will not share this with anyone else." Margaret was wide-eyed and more than happy to comply with Mother's request.

Mother took a rather large sip of her cocktail; we were into sidecars by now, "Dada told me nothing; not one thing other than I would have to suffer the obligations of marriage in order to have children. That was it.

I will tell you this, it's not a particularly pleasant experience. That's why there is only you Deborah. As far as how often? It's important for you to set those limits, and set them early on in the marriage. There can be no gray area."

And that was all Mother said on the subject.

Monday, July 29, 1940

Dad has another week of vacation. It's so great having him home. This was absolutely the hottest day yet. My clothes stuck to me all day. Never-the-less I was in the mood for a good game of bridge and some ice cold ale. Don came as I suspected he would. Mother and Dad almost beat us until we bid 6 diamonds and made it! Don was in a very good mood tonight – acting quite romantic, quite unusual for him too. Very nice!!

Tuesday, July 30, 1940

Another hot day, not as sticky as yesterday. I went out to dinner with Ruth. It was nice catching up. Don came just as we got home. We met him as we were walking up the steps. He was in a very queer mood – maybe he was tired. He certainly runs hot and cold. Anyway he made me awfully mad. We certainly are antagonistic towards each other. It was almost as though he were trying to pick a fight with me; but why come over just to do that?

We played bridge for a while. Ruth and I went down to meet Ruth's older brother Andrew's train. He is the same sophisticated bohemian New Yorker. He looked so handsome and dapper in his dark blue double-breasted suit. He is staying at the Lafayette Hotel. I'm not altogether certain why he's not staying with his parents.

Friday, August 2, 1940

We had Andrew and Ruth over for a spaghetti dinner this evening. Mother outdid herself as usual. Andrew had five helpings. He and Ruth brought over a bottle of red wine and a warm loaf of bread. He was humming as he ate. In the evening he told us all about the marvelous restaurants in New York and described the food in detail. He spoke of a dish with crepes, carrots and crabmeat with a delicate cream sauce that he had at Voisin on Park Avenue. Then there was Jack & Charlie's which always has the very best burgers. But his favorite is The Colony. He loves their crab stuffed lobster and seasonal vegetable. I started to hum just thinking about it.

Monday, August 5, 1940

Tonight was Don's birthday. Don wants me to come over and join the family for his birthday celebration. I think that's a big move on his part. We played bridge. His parents are darling and asked if I would play the piano for them. I was thrilled to do it.

We did start talking about politics. They are Roosevelt supporters. I had to hold my tongue. I'm hoping they change their minds. I'll have to be very careful as someday they very well might be my in-laws.

Don walked me home. We walked in the door just in time. Warm rain just poured down. It held him captive – simply perfect! We snuggled up on the davenport until it let up.

Thursday, August 8, 1940

I'm getting Friday off so I can go to the beach. Uncle George and Aunt Milly rented a cottage right on the water. Heaven! Carol and Laura are so excited about my staying for an extended weekend.

Mother and Dad drove me and we made great time. I had a swim as soon as I got there. The sun was shining all day and the sunset made my heart just soar. We had cocktails on the beach while we watched the day drift down into the lake.

The girls and I slept out on the screened-in porch. We could hear the crickets and the waves and smell the cinnamon smell of the sand. Oh, it was delightful. I woke up around 2:00 a.m. and sat on the steps looking up at the stars. It was nice to have some quiet time to myself. I don't ever mind being alone. I might be alone, but I'm never lonely.

Sunday, August, 11, 1940

Around 1:30 in the morning Ruth and I decided to go swimming a la nude. I'm so glad she came up for the night. Aunt Milly went down to the beach with us as a guard. There were a million stars in the night sky. Space and time seemed very infinite. We could see the tip of Aunt Milly's cigarette burning in the dark while she sat in a lawn chair on the beach waiting and guarding. She said when the light went out and she was finished with her cigarette it would be time for us to come in.

Monday, August 12, 1940

Don came over and we played bridge with Mother and Dad. I don't know what Don was wearing but did it smell dreamy! When we are sitting around the card table I often wonder if in a few years from now Don will be my husband? I know Dad likes and respects Don and he'd love to have a male presence in the family.

Chuck came over and spoiled a perfectly good evening. This is the second time he's done that and it's twice too many to suit me. He just loves to spoil things especially anything where I'm concerned.

Thursday, August 13, 1940

It has been a long time since I have said anything about the war. The blitzing against England has started. There are fierce aerial assaults but the English are bearing up well under them. They are bombing Germany every day. The Italians are doing their bit against the English.

Nan and I went to the movies and saw *Four Sons*. Don Ameche was perfect in it. It was another anti-German movie. It was very sad but it is good propaganda for this country.

Saturday, August 17, 1940

I had my hair done in a new way. I look more mature. I'm going to keep it this way for a while. I got the curse today. I feel dragged out – just when I wanted to feel good too.

We heard Willkie's acceptance speech while getting dressed for dinner. I met Dad and Don at the Saturn Club about quarter to seven. Mother joined us a little later as she was having her hair done. She looked so beautiful and elegant walking in. We really should belong here. Ruth's parents sponsored us for the evening.

Don was worse today than yesterday. He gets in these moods and it's so difficult to read him. Mother and Dad noticed his odd attitude as well. I'll just have to soldier on with this relationship as it builds.

Monday, August 19, 1940

Today is Carol's seventeenth birthday. I can't believe it. It hardly seems possible. I gave her Revlon nail polish and lipstick to match which she's been wanting for a long time. We all went to the movies to see *The Ramparts We Watch*. It is a picture about Americans for Americans. It shows all phases of life in this country during the first world war years. It was very stirring; carried a message.

I took Carol to the Statler for a cocktail. I told her to order something very sophisticated to celebrate her emerging into adulthood. She of course ordered a side car. When I got home I thought a great deal about the picture when I went to bed. I hope America does wake up in time to repel a Nazi invasion.

Thursday, August 22, 1940

Mother, Nan, Ruth and I played bridge tonight. We discussed Hitler's war and our preparedness in the United States including Wendell Willkie, Ambassador Bullett etc. We all got very incensed at the Germans. We all agree that our country will eventually be at war with Germany – how soon is problematic.

It's damn cool for August. I sat on the porch and had a cigarette. I got to thinking about all of us kids. If this conscription bill goes through Don will probably be in a training camp next summer. We may be in war by then, and I may be rolling bandages.

The British Isles may be completely demolished, but then again they might win. Oh God! I pray that they win. God! What a future to look into!

Saturday, August 24, 1940

Don and I went bowling with Sally and Lloyd. I broke 100 for the first time in my life. I got 107 as my score. After that we went to some joint with a floor show out in South Park district. I bought the first round of drinks. We all started to sing and the owner came over to our table. We thought he was going to ask us to stop. It was grand when he decided to join in.

We took Sally home and then we three went to Mann's. Don had an awful lot to drink. I wish he wouldn't be such a slave to it. I got in at 4 a.m. Don is quite romantic lately.

Tuesday, August 27, 1940

Don and I decided to have a party, and I certainly put in a hell of a day arranging for it. I am so mad at Don I could spit fire. Here I am all alone planning the party, and he absolutely runs out on me. He has dates for three nights in succession and will try to manage to get over here. Also he wants to ask some other drunk to the party who I don't know at all.

Sally and Lloyd came over tonight to help me. For a couple I haven't seen in a long time they are being so kind and helpful. Don should take a page from Lloyd's book. They are damn mad at Don too. Really, there are going to be so many outsiders at this party that it's not going to be like the old ones at all.

Saturday, August 31, 1940

What a nerve wracking day this was. I had to show three houses this morning then get home to help mother prepare for the party. What a dear she is, always pitching in.

Don brought his drunk friend as I suspected he would. I was emptying ashtrays, picking up dishes, changing records and trying to be a cordial hostess at the same time. I don't believe I had more than three drinks all evening.

Last guest left at 4:10 a.m. I dragged myself to bed. I knew I would make myself get up in time to help Mother clean up in the morning.

Sunday, September 1, 1940

Don, what am I going to do with him? He's such a dear, but he drinks so much! He gets awful lines on his face, and his complexion is becoming rather ruddy. I worry about him so. Dad said some men need Dutch courage to be in social situations. At this age he said it can be harmless and a sign of growing pains. But he added it can grow into a very bad habit.

Tuesday, September 3, 1940

I went downtown to dinner and a show with Bee and Nan. I'll have to call Margaret sup soon. I know she's been working very hard at the hospital. She's such a dedicated nurse.

I wore my new green outfit, and we had lobster at Lorenza's on Chestnut Street. It was excellent.

Boom Town, with Clark Gable, Spencer Tracy and Claudette Colbert, was swell. I find that I have to make myself breathe when Clark Gable comes on the screen. He truly takes my breath away.

Great Britain has been at war one year. As things stand now the British are certainly resisting Nazi air attacks. Britain is also raiding Germany all the time. Don was here while I was out; nice to know those things.

Thursday, September 5, 1940

Surprise! Don called me for a date. He was in sort of a funny mood though. When he picked me up he didn't seem to have a plan for the evening. We stopped at Coles and one other place and then came home. What kind of date was that supposed to be? I'm really going to have to have a talk with him about his dating style.

I'm so used to this getting in late stuff, the gift of youth.

The war is going swell. England is really doing plenty, and I guess Adolph really knows he's up against something. Our defense is being hurried up. President Roosevelt traded our 50 obsolete destroyers to England for land rights on British bases in Bermuda, Bahamas, Newfound land etc.

Sunday, September 8, 1940

I took a well-deserved nap this afternoon. I need to catch up on my sleep. Mother and I saw Bette Davis and Charles Boyer in *All This and Heaven Too*. It was so exquisitely done, truly a masterpiece. Bette is so finished and Boyer, well you can't say enough about him. I think he's short though.

We went over to the Marvins after the show. They have a new radio and get London direct.

Tuesday, Sept 10, 1940

Ruth and I called Margaret up and asked if she'd like to go to the Peter Stuyvesant Room for cocktails. She said it was perfect timing as she had the evening off and would love to kick up her heals a bit.

Perfect timing was right! We ran into Don while we were there. Don was a dear and offered to take me home. The girls didn't seem to mind my leaving with him. We girls have to be understanding that way. Men come first.

We went to Coles and had a few more cocktails. Don was real sweet after a while. It takes him time to warm up. We didn't get home until 4 a.m. He kissed me goodbye very tenderly and that was that.

I had told him about how Ruth and I had gone to Niagara Falls earlier in the day – the Canadian side. It was all barbed wire around vantage spots and soldiers were all over the place. I wonder if that turned his mood?

Wednesday, September 11, 1940

I felt very queer and slightly sad this morning. I've felt this way for three summers now; every time Don has left. He left at 8:00 a.m. for New York. I'll never know whether he was here last night because Mother and Dad weren't home.

I have decided to give up smoking and drinking until holiday time. I think my nerves will benefit. This summer has been quite a hectic one as far as late hours and imbibing is concerned.

Nan came over tonight and we played bridge for a couple of hours. She and Robert are going strong. At least someone has a steady love life.

Friday, September 13, 1940

Mother's dear friend Mrs. Miller is in town this weekend. She lives in Washington, D.C. What an exciting place to live at this time in history. I sat in the kitchen with Mother and Mrs. Miller and had some tea. I was so thrilled when Mrs. Miller said I should come and visit some time and she would take me to see all of the places worth seeing. Gee! It all sounds so wonderful that it doesn't seem possible that it will ever happen. I pray that nothing interferes and that she doesn't forget. She did seem rather enthused.

I can't believe it, but Don asked me to the movies. It was an anti-Nazi picture so of course we enjoyed it.

Saturday, September 14, 1940

Mother woke me up at 1:00 in the afternoon because Chuck of all people was at the door. I came down in my house coat and slippers. I have to say he just gets better and better looking. When I see him I get a rush of feelings remembering his expert technique at love making. I guess he'll never stop coming here. He stayed for lunch at Mother's insistence: cold chicken salad and brownies made him hum all through lunch. I kissed him on the cheek when he left. He has to work tonight so he didn't invite me out.

It seems funny not to be going out on Saturday night any more. It seems like all of my friends are away. But I do need the rest. Mother and Dad went out tonight.

I sat alone by the fire listening to the radio. All my memories came back to me. It's perfect to sit and dream about times that may never come again. Don seems more remote and far away than ever. If I don't hear from him soon I'll know it's because was I so sassy to him last week.

Was there some divine reason for Chuck to come over today? What plan does God have for all of us? I wish I knew.

It began to rain, and I spent the rest of the night knitting. I had the radio on to keep me company. London is standing up under terrific aerial bombardment. The Germans hope to break down the morale of the people and invade. They are up against something tough, and they know it. Buckingham Palace was damaged by bombs yesterday. It's all so harrowing to think of.

Monday, September 16, 1940

The Nazis are savage in their attacks. The greatest city in the world is being destroyed. It hardly seems possible.

Willkie made his first campaign speech today. It was vigorous and forceful. He is wonderful!

The draft bill was signed today by President Roosevelt. All young me between the ages of 21 and 36 must register for military training. It starts October 16.

Mother and I saw Laurence Olivier and Greer Garson in *Pride & Prejudice.* It was grand! She is so beautiful and I love him so. I could listen to him read the phone book and be enthralled.

Wednesday, September 18, 1940

The war is hot. RAF bombers drew 300 Nazi planes today in fire battle. Adolph is changing plans about invasion, at least that's what Washington thinks. He must be mighty surprised over the thing.

Nan was so kind; she brought me over some red yarn for a sweater. She got me started on it tonight. I'm so crazy about knitting. I stayed in to listen to Wendell Willkie broadcast from Los Angeles. It was before a crowd of 80,000; it was such a swell speech. He assails the New Deal every time he speaks. This is a man who knows what he's talking about. He's got my vote!

Sunday, September 22, 1940

The *New York Times* today reprinted their editorial announcing their choice of Wendell Willkie for president. It's the first editorial I have ever read.

Bee was over tonight. I was so pleased she stayed for dinner. We have veered off of our usual topic of discussion, sex of course. War is on our minds more than ever now. The Germans sank a non-combat vessel on its way to Canada with mostly children on it. That will create a great deal of feeling on this side of the Atlantic.

Wednesday, September 25, 1940

The foreign situation is getting tricky. Germany has made an agreement with Japan. The battle is to keep us interested so Hitler can finish off England.

I couldn't believe it; John came over tonight. He wants to start a Willkie youth club. By chance he and Chuck arrived at the same time. I said yes to the club for sure! If we all pull together we can put this man in office. John gave me a Willkie election campaign pin. It's actually a key. I will keep it always.

Chuck is so nice lately. I have a date with him Friday night. I'm really looking forward to it. I'm trying to decide what to wear. I hope we go to the movies and maybe we could get a sandwich at Coles. That's such a fun place to go. It has such a cozy feeling. I don't go to The Wishing Well or Mann's because Don and I would go there, too many memories.

There is a chill in the air. I am going to miss the summer weather. I do love the changing leaves.

Friday, September 27, 1940

I just knew that something would go wrong with my date with Chuck. His parents wouldn't let him have the car, and he had a row with them. I went and had my hair done for the occasion too!

John came over with all of the work he wants me to do for the Willkie campaign. Oh, and I guess our play isn't coming off. Our director, Mrs. Yoffee, went to Florida for the winter. I certainly can't blame her. That's where I would like to be. As far as the Willkie campaign goes I'd rather invest my efforts there than a play. It is a grand feeling to know that you are working for a real American cause. Mr. Willkie's picture is on the cover of *Life* Magazine this week. It also contains a lot of his campaign strategy.

Monday, September 30, 1940

As I go to bed tonight I feel so much more heartened about Willkie's chances. In his speech in Detroit, he lashed out at political machines and named names. He's so brave! Mother and I get plenty excited listening to him, and I yelled like the audience at our radio. Dad told me to tone it down.

I talked to Nan tonight. She agrees with me that the election is the most important thing in our lives. We have decided to go to the Willkie rally Friday night. It is so important for us all to support this great man.

Wednesday, October 2, 1940

Our kitchen is being redecorated – done over in ivory. The wallpaper is darling. Mother has bought some chrome and ivory chairs to go with it.

Tonight Willkie lashed out at the New Deal's defense program. Boy! Did he say plenty. Every day I pray that he will win and save our country. I toss at night thinking about it.

Friday, October 4, 1940

Willkie's speech to labor last night was exceptionally good. I called for Nan and her sister, and we went to the Democratic rally for Willkie. Banbridge Colby, former Secretary of State under Woodrow Wilson spoke and he was grand! Also a democratic congressman from Pennsylvania, Robert Allen, and they lashed out against the New Deal and the President for his maneuvering of the third term nomination.

I couldn't help but cry over what is happening to our country.

Monday, October 7, 1940

I cried most of the day over what is happening to this country. The "New Dealers" have such control of this country that Willkie is fighting against great odds.

I went to my music appreciation class today. It's very informative. I enjoy learning about the complexities and subtle nuances of music. Music is such a healing tool. It soothes my beaten soul.

While I was at class I missed Willkie's speech from New Jersey. Mother told me all about it – the best yet according to her. The crowd went wild! He called Hague, Flynn, Kelly and Nash penny Hitlers who perpetuate Roosevelt into power. Plenty is coming out about the New Deal.

I got a swell letter from Tommy. He's still keen on me coming to Washington on vacation. I haven't heard from Mrs. Miller yet, but I know she'll come through. I would like to stay with her and save some money on hotel expenses. Mother doesn't want me staying in a hotel alone anyway.

How Washington must be alive with power!

Tuesday, October 8, 1940

Just when we all thought England was coming over Germany, the Nazis have resumed terrific aerial bombardments of London. The Far East situation is quite acute. Roosevelt seems to be doing his darndest to promote war.

Willkie answered letters over the radio tonight. He sounded very tired indeed. He is very courageous. I feel very sorry for him. I do hope he can make the American people see the light. It certainly will be terrible if we're in the war before the election. We're so totally unprepared (Something we have to thank the New Deal for.)

Oh, it's all a swell kettle of fish. The only honest person in the country is Willkie. But he'll probably be another martyr to the cause of democracy.

Chuck called and I refused a date with him Saturday night. I know it's our "anniversary," but I'm not in the mood for love.

I need to sort my life out. I have so much thinking to do. Someday I want to go to college. I know Dad doesn't want to foot the bill for it. It's so difficult for me to save large amounts of money. I just love to shop.

Sunday, October 13, 1940

It is a perfectly beautiful day. I took a ride to East Aurora to see the leaves change – I went all by myself. It was lovely having a quiet afternoon to myself. The colors were ablaze. I stopped at a roadhouse tavern and had an ale and sandwich – I liked spending time with Deborah.

The campaign has reached a new low. The democrats of New York City that is, the Negros have put out a smear pamphlet saying Willkie is pro-German. I think it is low and contemptible. Now I hate Roosevelt more than ever. He knows all about that stuff, and he's in a position to repudiate it and he doesn't! What kind of man is that?!

Ruth and I went to the Republican headquarters on Hertel Avenue. I had the man there spellbound by my speeches. They all thought I was a very good campaigner. I wish that I could meet Mr. Willkie. Just to speak with him one on one for even a moment would be such a thrill.

Tuesday, October 15, 1940

No words can really describe my feelings tonight. Mother, Dad and I called for Ruth and Nan. Memorial Auditorium was comfortably filled when we arrived. The parades were swell. The crowd overflowed the building. The whole surging mass of humanity rose in acclamation as Wendell Willkie himself came onto the platform. I cheered until I was almost sick. His speech was wonderful. At the end he did as always. He raised his arms above his head as if to say "I love you all so much, so much!"

Wednesday, October 16, 1940

All I could think of all day was last night. It is without parallel, the greatest thrill of my life. You've got to see Willkie to really appreciate him. The crowd last night was 22,000 in the auditorium and another 10,000 outside who couldn't get in. Boy am I thrilled that we were up close and personal with that magnetic man.

I'll never forget last night as long as I live – a spontaneous acclaim of a free people. Willkie seems to revitalize the audience with his vitality – Viva Willkie!!

Monday, October 28, 1940

Greece is at war with Italy. At least we have an ally for Great Britain. If only Turkey would jump in now everything would be swell.

Ambassador Kennedy just came back from England. He's going to make a speech tomorrow night. Roosevelt whined through his speech tonight. Willkie was simply swell. He got a terrific ovation down in Kentucky. The first thing he said was "My voice is husky; it never was golden." He never could have said anything more to the point.

Tuesday, October 29 1940

I got a letter from Don. As usual lately it was a lot about nothing.

Tonight was just about the limit. Joe Kennedy, Ambassador to England, spoke tonight on the war and for Roosevelt. It was absolutely the worst political trick I've ever heard of. Also, Miss Dorothy Thompson shredded John L. Lewis to bits for his stand to vote for Willkie. She is obviously a fanatic on the subject of war, and she doesn't want anyone who likes peace in the presidency. What kind of journalist is she!

Tuesday, November 5, 1940

The long awaited day is over. As I go to bed Roosevelt is way ahead of Willkie. My heart is so heavy. It is all turning out as I predicted. Willkie is doing well, but I guess the foreign situation is beating him. I feel so sorry for him. He put up such a noble and valiant fight. Well I'll never forget this campaign or Wendell Willkie.

During the night it got very cold and the wind blew hard – sort of an ill omen of the far reaching effects of the third term.

Sunday, November 10, 1940

The European war is getting more involved. The Greeks are giving the Italians hell. However, the worst is yet to come. The Russian foreign minister, Vyacheslav Molotov is on his way to Berlin. There will probably be another power added to the Russia- Berlin – Tokyo axis. If the Russians join up with Hitler it's going to be pretty awful. Our entry into the war seems imminent.

Thursday, November 14, 1940

I met Mother and Dad at Laube's Old Spain for a swell lobster dinner. I took them to Shea's to see Norma Shearer and Robert Taylor in *Escape*. It was a perfect copy of the book – had that same element of suspense. Oh, that Robert Taylor, he is so devastatingly handsome. I feel it in the pit of my stomach.

I called for Nan at 10:15 and dashed to the meeting at "Dac" Davenports. I met a lot of new kids there. We discussed war, the N.L.R.B (National Labor Relations Board) and possibilities of National Socialism. Our program, of course, is to uphold the principals of American democracy by continuing Wendell Willkie's course.

Thursday, November 21, 1940 Thanksgiving

I wore my new blue dress for the first time. We stopped at the Brown's before going to Uncle George and Aunty Milly's. They had a grand fire going in the fireplace and cocktails chilled and ready for us. We tried not to speak of the war, but it was difficult to avoid. Mrs. Brown had tears in her eyes when she gave me a hug good-bye. She said she is so worried for our youth and what our future holds.

It was a quiet ride in the car over to the Marvins, but it was quite different when we entered their welcoming and warm house. Carol and Laura ushered me into the living room and insisted I warm myself by the fire while Uncle George slipped a sidecar in my hand almost before I had a chance to get my arm out of my coat sleeve.

We had more cocktails before dinner. We had all of trimmings: imported Cointreau, cranberry sauce, creamed onions, nuts, plum pudding with brandy hard sauce, two turkeys, plenty of stuffing and mashed potatoes, lots of thick warm gravy, turnip and butternut squash and an after dinner cordial called The Creature. It's made with dark red cherries and vodka. It sits in their attic for an entire year before it's ready to drink. It certainly was perfect to end the dinner.

The candles were lit and the lights were dimmed as I sat and looked around the table at all the beautiful happy faces with my glass of Creature in my hand. I couldn't help but look into the future and wonder if next Thanksgiving will be as happy as this one.

Monday, November 25, 1940

Mother and Dad and I got a laugh out of an article in the paper. It seems that some of the members of the Willkie youth club were investigated for "subversive" activities. However, all suspicions were unfounded.

There was just a committee meeting tonight. "Dac" has written an awesome rebuttal in Everybody's *Column* tonight to the letter asking Mr. Willkie's' clubs to step down. I can't wait to read it. We expect to see it in the paper tomorrow night.

Tuesday, November 26, 1940

Sure enough "Dac's" answer was in the paper tonight, and it was plenty good and a forthright answer.

This was an exciting day at work. Bud became a father of a baby girl at 9:30 a.m. His wife Roberta is doing fine and so is the baby. Bud passed out cigars as it always happens.

It occurred to me that I rarely write about work anymore. It's not nearly as interesting to me as it was.

I added more pages to Willkie's scrapbook. I know it will be decades before it is finished, for his career will continue through the years and he will have a clear influence on the future of the United States.

Monday, December 2, 1940

I'm reading *Tree of Liberty* by Elizabeth Page. It's very slow at work. No one buys homes in December. It is nice being able to read at work all day.

When I left work I went to *The Sample Shop* and found a nice bargain; a rose wool dress with maroon buttons and belt. I got it for $5.00, formerly $7.95.

I played bridge with Bee, Nan and Mother tonight. We didn't speak of war – we need to let our minds rest from it.

Friday, December 6, 1940

I woke up to find more snow. Driving is terrific these days. It is the coldest for this time since 1916. I had my hair done. Nan and Ruth came over to spend the evening. Dad has recovered from his cold sufficiently to mix us some cocktails. We had an awfully nice time talking and playing bridge.

I have a new record Handel *Largo*. It is beautiful and one of my favorites. *Meditation* is on the other side.

Tuesday, December 10, 1940

I went to Margaret's for lunch. Those nurses have odd hours. She prepared a nice lunch – toasted cheese and bacon sandwiches, canned peaches, cookies and tea.

Mother and I went downtown to see Bette Davis in *The Letter*. The first lady of the screen was at her best tonight. I don't see how she can perform so vividly, so realistically. The movie was about a woman who married a man she didn't love and murdered a man she did love, but who didn't love her. What a story!

Thursday, December 12, 1940

Lord Lothian, Britain's Ambassador to the United States, died today in Washington of uremic poisoning. He was a Christian Scientist, I guess. Anthony Eden is being suggested to replace him.

The British were trying to knock Italy right out of the war and from all reports, it looks as if they were doing it.

I addressed my Christmas cards tonight. It makes me feel good to have that much out of the way.

Monday, December 16, 1940

I wrote a letter to *Everybody's Column* in *The Buffalo News*. I doubt if it will be published because everything is about war now and mine is about Willkie. "Dac" wrote a very good article called "The Case Against F.D.R." In it he describes how he was for Roosevelt until the night Willkie came to Buffalo then he changed his mind; this show the power of Willkie's personality and his convincing speech.

Roosevelt is back from his Caribbean Cruise. I wonder if any action will begin now? How can he go on a cruise at this time? We need our leader here taking charge and making us all feel safe. This is no time for a vacation. This is why we know we can count on Willike.

I wake up every morning so nervous, wondering what happened in the world as I slept.

Friday, December 20, 1940

When I got home from work Dad told me that some woman had called to congratulate me on my article about Willkie in *Everybody's Column* tonight. I called her back. She's a librarian on the Stock Exchange and we had a very interesting talk. Then the floodgate opened up, and the phone kept on ringing. Friends and family were all very proud of me. How exciting to have your words move people in such a profound way.

Sunday, December 22, 1940

I had a very interesting talk with "Dac" last night that I find rather disturbing. He seems to think there is a Communist among our club members. If this is so it is quite an exciting thing. We've got to be plenty careful in all of our doings, publicly and privately.

Mother and Dad went out to dinner with the Browns to the Peter Stuyvesant Room. I went over to see Carol and Laura, and they invited me to stay for dinner and the night. We had a great time sitting in front of the Christmas tree remembering Christmastime when we were young.

We didn't stay up very late. I have to get up early for work tomorrow, and I also have some more shopping to do. This is such a busy time of year. My calendar is so full of things to do.

Tuesday, December 24, 1940

This is sure going to be a green Christmas. It is very mild out. I only had to work a half a day today. I ironed my underwear and cleaned out my closet for any new gifts coming my way tomorrow.

I got a Haig & Haig bottle for Dad and red roses for Mother. Uncle George came over for a glass of cheer with us. Laura, Carol and I went to church at 11:00. Last year I went with Don

We went over to the Marvins for cocktails and appetizers. When we came home I sat in the living room all alone looking at the tree with presents under it. How nice, it began to snow.

Wednesday, December 25, 1940

Mother is so happy over her coffee table, lamps and cocktail tray that Dad bought her. I helped him pick them out of course. I got a gorgeous negligée and suitcase, also a blue cardigan and underwear galore. Bee came over and gave me two Strauss Waltz records and Wagner's *Ride of the Valkyries*.

We had a delicious meal as always. This year seems so strange. War is looming, and we don't know what our future holds. We celebrate being together, but there is a sense of fear in our hearts.

Sunday, December 29, 1940

Tonight the President of the United States made an important speech not only to our country but to the world. It was a fine speech, and it showed that the axis could not bluff us. The best thing Mr. Roosevelt said was "I do not believe that the axis powers will win this war."

Monday, December 30, 1940

Roosevelt's speech has drawn mostly praise, but the isolationists in Congress are all steamed up over it. England thought it was wonderful along with Greece and Turkey and China.

The German and Italian powers tore the speech apart in denunciation.

Tuesday, December 31, 1940

Nan, Ruth, Margaret, Bee and I celebrated New Year's Eve over here. At midnight we opened champagne and drank to the end of the war.

This year that has faded to a close has been an all-important year for world history. France was conquered, bombing in London, worst destruction in all history, the Greeks took the offensive against Italy; so very much devastation to deal with. In this country we saw the rise of Wendell Willkie and the re-election of Franklin Roosevelt to a third term.

We are a strong country and good will always triumph over evil.

We searched, and searched through all of Deborah's many boxes left behind, but to no avail. Deborah's diary for 1941 could not be found. What a year to have lost. There were so many questions and relationships left unanswered. Thank goodness there was one person left who could help fill in the missing months. I baked a batch of cookies and took them over to Laura's lovely little home where she now lived alone. Her family raised and on their own, and her dear husband of over 40 years having passed away, she made a comfortable life for herself with her two cats, her beautiful, lush garden and frequent visits from children, grandchildren, great-grandchildren, friends and neighbors. She put on a pot of tea, and I brought out my pad and pen. Laura, very sharp and articulate at 91, told me what she could recall of that missing year.

"*1941 was a very difficult year for our country, the world and for Deborah personally. I vividly remember on December 8, 1941 President Roosevelt spoke to the world. I'll never forget his voice when he said, "Yesterday, a date which will live in infamy," and then he went on to tell of the attack on Pearl Harbor to our horror. This was a year of decisions for our Deborah and all of her friends. Twenty-one is when you are no longer a child; you are a full- fledged adult, but there are still some childlike qualities that linger at that age.*

Deborah always loved Buffalo, but there was something inside of her that yearned to travel, to see as much of life and the world as she could. She was always a very passionate person. She truly loved everything: food, movies, fragrances, seasons, holidays, clothes, shopping, and cocktails and of course boys.

1941 saw a lot of change for our country, our city and our own personal lives. All of those beautiful boys who filled Deborah's house made big changes of their own.

Don up and married Mary Ruth, the girl he had met at Duke. Deborah was shocked beyond belief and consolation. She was in deep despair for weeks. I remember it was in June, and Deborah had longed to be a June bride. Don moved back to Buffalo with Mary Ruth and lived with his parents. They stayed with his parents for quite a while, and I believe they had a baby in 1942. I remember Deborah telling me years and years later that he had stopped by just like old times one night when Mary Ruth was at the movies with his mother. Deborah said she had been cool and as polite as she could be to this young man who only months earlier had been making love to her in this very doorway. She didn't invite him in. As she stood at the door after his short visit she said "This is your last visit at this house," and abruptly shut the door.

That was indeed the very last time she ever saw him. She had heard through the grapevine that he divorced after 20 years of marriage, married again and divorced again. After that she had lost track him.

Now, as for Chuck, ah, dear Chuck. I liked him, he had a nice face and a nice smile, and he was always kind to me. He joined the Air Force and returned a decorated hero. He went back to school and earned a law degree. Someone told me that he married a girl he met at the law office where he worked. They had seven children and opened up their own practice. Four of their seven children became attorneys and also joined the firm. I'd see ads for their law offices on billboards every now and then.

Years after he passed away his oldest daughter wrote an editorial for My View in The Buffalo News. I recall how touched I was with her loving regard for her father. She spoke of his kindness and his dedication to help others and devotion to his family and community. I clipped it out and sent it to Deborah.

When Chuck enlisted in 1941, Deborah was in New York at the time. She never had a chance to say goodbye. When he died I sent her his obituary. She called me and was a bit teary. She said what she wrote in her diary way back when was still true – she would always consider him her first great romance.

John never married. I recall that he became somewhat of a drifter, showing up now and then in Buffalo. I'd run into him at stores or just in passing. He never seemed to shake his cynical outlook on life. He carried it with him. I don't know what ever happened to him later on. I never saw him after the mid-50s.

Bee became a research scientist in the field of coronary care. She never married. She then returned to school to become a heart surgeon. You know, I always thought Bee was somewhat in love with Deborah. All of those intimate talks they would have.

I know Ruth got married and lived a very happy life from what I know. I'm not really sure about Margaret. I know she stayed with nursing. Ginger, that girl who Deborah didn't really care for, now there's a story. She moved to Los Angeles and became an actress of all things. She was rather successful. I saw her in several Twilight Zones and she was on As the World Turns, an old soap opera. She was in a few movies too, but I can't remember what they were.

It's rather amusing, but whenever I would mention to Deborah that Ginger was in a movie or on t.v., she would immediately change topics. Deborah always fancied herself as actress material. Her teacher once told her how remarkable her voice was and how she would be able to project her voice on stage. She encouraged her to pursue a career in theater. I think she might have given it a shot had it not been for the war.

Deborah's house on Starin Ave became so quiet in 1941; I think it became unbearable for her. She became *rather discontented with her job at the real-estate office. It became dull and not terribly challenging for her. When she moved to Washington it came as no surprise to Carol and me. We knew she would never stay in Buffalo and feel content. It was sad for all of us to see her leave, but we were so proud of her. We knew she would be a great success in her career. Over the years I had often wondered if the war hadn't happened how would all of those young people's lives have turned out differently?*

Oh, and you know how she would go to Coles with the boys so often? Well, on Christmas Eve 1949 Deborah was home for the holidays. She rounded up the gang, and we all met at Coles to celebrate Joe and I getting engaged. We all sat in the main bar area at the big round table. It was quite a celebration."

Epilogue
A Heart Surrenders

December 13, 1998

Deborah's nurse was adjusting the shades in her room and mentioned that there was a storm coming. Deborah could see the quiet, steady fall of soft white snow coming down with movie scene slow motion. Her nurse's name was Ruth and reminded Deborah a bit of her friend Ruth from Buffalo. Not so much in the way she looked, but in her smile and kindness. She had a natural ease in the way she moved about the room and was so gentle with Deborah's possessions.

Deborah was relieved to have a private room. The hospital is no place to make friends and engage in idle conversation. Her heart wouldn't be in it. As she looked out the window she felt a twinge of guilt for having sent Laura out on such a blustery night. The gentle snow had turned in to a harsh and unrelenting gale.

Laura was happy to do what she could for her cousin. Deborah, who had always been such a strong and impressive force in her life, now appeared frail and uncharacteristically resigned.

Laura easily found the simple watercolor painting of a street scene in Paris that Deborah has sent her out to get. When Laura found the painting at the foot of Deborah's bed at her condo, she remembered having seen it over the years. The unusual mix of cherry blossoms and roses climbing up a church wall always struck Laura as a strange combination. It wasn't a terribly good painting, and the subject matter appeared pedestrian for Deborah's refined and educated taste. It was hung in an almost ceremonial manner over her bureau with a candle beneath it in an empty 1943 Chianti bottle – obviously having been lit many times. Placed next to it were leather bound diaries dating from 1937 to 1945 with a sealed enveloped propped up against them. Deborah's unmistakable thick black script had written Laura - **To be opened upon my death.**

Laura slipped the letter into her handbag and lifted the painting from the wall. The outline showed that it had hung there for many years. She carefully wrapped it in the brown paper that Deborah had left for her on the kitchen table, and placed the package at the front door so as not to forget it.

Laura realized as she walked about Deborah's home that it had been a long time since she had visited her. Children, husband, friends and family obligations had to come first. Yet Deborah always made time to come to Buffalo for a visit once a year during the summer.

As Laura stood in Deborah's living room she felt odd staying there without her. However, there was so much to remind her of old times that it began to comfort her. It was like walking into the old house on Starin Avenue, the dining room set and corner hutch, the kitchen table with three chairs and one for a guest, was in the small kitchen placed next to the window. She had even kept the old davenport. It had been re-upholstered many times, but the bones of it were still there. Laura had to smile when she noticed the elaborate red and green Oriental rug with the hidden stain of cocktail sauce from the New Year's Eve party in 1938. She had tried so hard to clean it up before anyone could notice. Laura let out a sigh when she thought of how many Christmas Eves, Easter dinners, Thanksgivings and countless birthday parties and family celebrations had been spent with these simple pieces of furniture. They all brought back so many fond memories.

Laura leaned against the doorway of Deborah's bedroom. There was Deborah's bedroom set that both she and Carol adored. It had always seemed so elegant to the girls, and now it had grown old and worn over the many years that Deborah had been unable to part with it. Deborah would sit at her dressing table with her sets of Evening in Paris cologne, her many bottles of nail polish and face creams surrounding her. She would primp for a dance, apply her nightly ritual of cream to her hands and face, or jot down the days' occurrences in her leather-bound diaries. It was a scene Laura had watched over and over again while growing up.

Deborah's condo was filled with memories from Buffalo. They must have been a great comfort to her, as she never replaced any of them.

When Laura arrived at the hospital Ruth gestured her over to the nurse's station. She explained that Deborah was just about to doze off and suggested that if she found her asleep for Laura to come back in the morning. Laura peeked in and could see that Deborah had indeed drifted off. She quietly unwrapped the painting her cousin had so anxiously been waiting for and hung it on the wall at the foot of her bed to greet her first thing in the morning. She gave her dear cousin a light kiss on her forehead and quietly shut the door.

During the night Deborah awoke to the sound of soft Christmas music playing in the room next door occupied by an older gentleman who would often play his radio very quietly at night. How appropriate for *I'll be Home for Christmas* to be playing. Deborah looked up and saw her painting bathed in the light of the moon; what a dear Laura was to bring it to her. Deborah smiled and shut her eyes while Bing Crosby crooned her to sleep:

I'll be home for Christmas
You can plan on me
Please have snow and mistletoe
And presents on the tree

Christmas Eve will find me
Where the love light gleams
I'll be home for Christmas
If only in my dreams

Laura received the call early in the morning. Ruth was very kind and quite sincere with her sympathy. Deborah was a patient she would always remember. Laura hung up the phone and sat quietly on the davenport. She noticed an unseasonal hint of lilacs, and her thoughts went to her sister, Carol, who had died at the young age of 42, her parents, aunts and uncles who had long since passed, and now Deborah. Deborah the adventurer who had left Buffalo at the age of 21 to live and work in Washington D.C. to help win the war. There was no doubt in Laura's mind that she most definitely made a significant contribution towards those ends. Reaching deep into her purse, she pulled out the letter Deborah had left for her and carefully opened it.

My Dearest Laura,

I have just finished a small, but delicious Thanksgiving feast. It pales in comparison to the meals we would share when surrounded by family years ago, but it will have to do. I am alone, but not lonely. I have lived a single life very unlike yours with your husband, children, grandchildren and lovely home. You have shared a life with the man who you have loved for over forty years.

I am certain that you have considered my life adventurous and fascinating, and perhaps if you were to be honest with yourself, a little lonely and passionless. You have always been such a dear sweet cousin to me; however, I felt it unwise to confide in you some of the details of my life. Please do not feel shut out. As I have said, we lead very different lives, followed different paths.

I did confide in Carol as she at times faced some of the difficult decisions that I had to make. The diaries before you are yours to do with as you please. They are the writings of a young girl becoming a young woman during a very turbulent time in our county's history. There may be passages that shock your delicate senses, but in respect to the times they are quite tame. War years are like none other.

My heart has traveled a long and varied course – it is tired now. I realize it is, as Mother always said since the day I was born, a broken heart. It has rallied many times but is a tired soldier and needs permission to go quietly into that good night.

I believe I will not see Christmas, not on this earthly plain. I will spend it I know with Mother, Dad, Grammie, Dada, friends and family who have all made this journey, and hopefully one very special soldier waiting with open and forgiving arms.

Much love to you dear, dear cousin.
Deborah

My mother-in-law, Susanne Marvin Flynn (Laura) at the book launch at The Saturn Club of Buffalo for my first book, Cherry Blossom Diaries Buffalo to Washington 1942 -1945.

Mary Mullett-Flynn

Is a writer and watercolor artist in Buffalo, New York and owns a small shop, Back of the Moon: Gifts & Gallery in Wilson, New York, showcasing her moon inspired paintings and whimsical gifts. She has conducted writing workshops at the Chautauqua Institute, Just Buffalo Literary Center, and The Albright Knox Art Gallery working with children through their, A Picture's Worth a Thousand Words program, pairing docents with writers. She lives in Kenmore, New York with her husband Patrick, son, Evan and puppies' lily and Ella. Please feel free to contact Ms. Mullett-Flynn at moonpaintings@gmail.com with your insight and inquiries.

Lilac Blossom Diaries
The Buffalo Years 1937-1941
Mary Mullett-Flynn
Please leave a review on Amazon
Contact info: moonpaintings@gmail.com

Made in the USA
Middletown, DE
10 June 2016